PULP
Literature

Pulp Literature Press

Issue No. 19, Summer 2018

Pulp Literature Press, Publisher; Jennifer Landels, Managing Editor; Melanie Anastasiou, Acquisitions Editor; Susan Pieters, Story Editor; Jessica Fabrizius, Assistant Editor; Daniel Cowper, Poetry Editor; Amanda Bidnall, Copy Editor; Mary Rykov, Proofreader; Kris Sayer, Graphic Designer. For advertising rates, direct inquiries to info@pulpliterature.com.

Cover painting, *After the Tsunami*, by Tais Teng. Illustrations for 'Blue Skies Over Nine Isles' by Hugh Henderson. Illustrations for *Allaigna's Song: Aria* by JM Landels. All other illustrations by Mel Anastasiou.

Pulp Literature: ISSN 2292-2164 (Print), ISSN 2292-2172 (Online), Issue No. 19, Summer 2018.

Published quarterly by Pulp Literature Press, 8540 Elsmore Road, Richmond, BC, Canada V7C 2A1, pulpliterature.com, at $15.00 per copy. Annual subscription $50.00 in Canada, $66.00 in continental USA, $82.00 elsewhere. Printed in Victoria, BC, Canada, by First Choice Books/Victoria Bindery. Copyright © 2018 Pulp Literature Press. All stories and works of art copyright © 2018, as per their authors bylines.

Pulp Literature Press gratefully acknowledges the support of the Canada Council for the Arts.

Pulp Literature is a proud member of the Magazine Association of BC and Magazines Canada.

TABLE OF CONTENTS

FROM THE PULP LIT PULPIT

Advent's Arrival

On Bowen Island, at Mel's cedar-beamed house overlooking the Georgia Strait, where five years ago Pulp Literature was conceived, there is a wall of books — lovely aging paperbacks, well thumbed and loved, many of them science fiction books now considered classics. Mel is an avid reader. So when Mel, in her role as acquisitions editor, found a speculative novel that made her go, 'Wow', Jen and Sue stepped in to take a look. Thus, we are happy to announce the launch of Michael Kamakana's first novel, *Advent*, excerpted in this issue.

We have high expectations for all our stories and poems at Pulp Literature, and as we expand into novel publication, we are keeping those same standards. Read, enjoy, and spread the good news: *Pulp Literature* continues to print great reads for the price of a beer!

Jen, Mel, & Sue
Pulp Literature Press

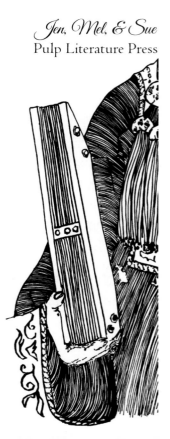

We lead with a tight punch in an excerpt from *Advent*, **Michael Kamakana's** SF stunner of a debut novel, which opens with "When the aliens came it was not what we expected." Need we say more? Another debut, **Jasmin Nyack**'s 'Five Minutes', has a totally different and hilarious take on alien invasion.

Spencer Stevens travels to the age of steam in the newest Seven Swans novella by **Mel Anastasiou**, *The Machineries of Progress*, and we take a trip of a different kind in **Maria Pascualy**'s poem, 'First Date'.

Alex Reece Abbott's short story, 'My Brother Paulie', is a sharp study of an altered state of being, and 'Guardian', by **Susan Pieters**, turns personal safety into claustrophobia and morphs danger into desire.

We progress and evolve in new ways in **Richard O'Brien**'s 'The Slade Transmutation', another evolution occurs in 'Ordinary', by **Sylvia Stopforth**, and Allaigna adapts to her transformation from runaway to fugitive in the latest instalment of *Allaigna's Song: Aria* by **JM Landels**.

The grotesquery of flies has us itching for a swatter in **James Norcliffe**'s 'He has this thing', while **Charity Tahmaseb**'s 'Potato Bug War' has us rooting for the pests to survive.

Bumblebee contest winner **RS Wynn** weaves five tight narratives into one flash fiction piece titled 'Lullaby, Valentine, Paper

Crane' alongside the Surrey International Writers' Conference Storyteller Award runner-up, 'Towing the Mustang' by **Keltie Zubko**.

Last year, in the first chapter of *Blue Skies Over Nine Isles* by **Joseph Stilwell** and **Hugh Henderson**, we left Maxwell facing a threat and several questions. In the second chapter, Max gets a hand up, but don't think for a second that his rescuer is giving him a handout.

ADVENT

Michael Kamakana

Michael Kamakana *is a Calgary-based novelist with a talent for storytelling that holds readers rapt. He is a prolific writer who works almost non-stop to get his work out of his head and into print. From our first read of* Advent, *we knew we had something special. Here for you, a stand-alone excerpt of the novel* Advent, *coming soon from Pulp Literature Press. Find out more and pre-order your copy at pulpliterature.com/advent.*

$\mathcal{A}$DVENT

$\mathcal{R}$ESET

When the aliens came it was not what we expected. We did not even realize that human history had come to an end. We wanted to believe that the aliens were just a new aspect of our human world. We wanted to believe that whatever was to happen, we humans were the central protagonists. We were shocked but quickly adjusted to this advent, even as we necessarily saw it as a radical change in our human story with unsuspected new characters. In our sense of history the aliens were long expected. We wondered how anyone could have ever imagined persisting secrecy, could have ever imagined this advent would not change everything in our human story. We could think in terms of narratives. We could imagine what we could not before imagine. We were ready for this adventure. We had seen the movies. We were ready to reset or adjust to this new feature of our human lives. We thought that somehow we would continue, that no matter how the aliens were disposed to us, we adaptable humans would find common qualities, find logic, find love, find hatred, find some meaning to this encounter. We were proud, we were fearful, we were tentative, we thought ourselves at the beginning of a wondrous new history and not simply at the end of human history. Some people were happily amazed, though this reaction did not long persist. Some people were immediately fearful. Some people were joyous. Some people were in dislocating shock and unable to react either way. Some people were ecstatic to be visited by elder beings of another evolution that knew so many, many, magical tech. We had in those first days, first months, first years, many and often conflicting ideas of what they want, what we want, what this all means. Some people saw the aliens as aliens. Some people who were religious claimed these aliens were actually gods or emissaries or potentates or facilitators of their god or gods. Some people who were atheists claimed this was proof that the universe, if not the world, was a natural creation. Some people lost their faith, some people gained a new faith. Some people tried to form a religion around the aliens, but there was nothing we could call miracle, judgment, grace, damnation — in fact, nothing humans had previously called religious. Some people said we defined religious experience, religious sentiment, too narrowly and typically in our post-industrial way. Some people said we were lucky to see the inevitable triumph of the true spiritual world, the true church, the last church. Some people saw great promise in the aliens, some great fear. Our merely human leaders could only hold their breath, hold it long and longer, until finally collapsing with piercing mental anguish. Some people lost their minds and acted out their madness. Some people insisted they were now possessed by these aliens, excusing fantastic and horrific crimes, revealing by their acts just how alien were these others. We were all human now, truly. We were ready to discover just how human we all were and what that status meant. We were human, but no one knew that when the aliens came our proud claims, our human insistence, our human naming was no longer ours to make. We humans perhaps all wanted the same things, food for our families, shelter from the rain or snow or burning sun and scouring sandstorms, care for our elders, a future for our children. We simply had fatal disagreements on how our desires were needs, how desires were ordered in importance as spiritually deferred or materially immediate, how we humans could best satisfy our needs, but such conflicts had always been so before the aliens came and was not so different now. We saw that the impoverished subcontinental weavers of our shirts, our trousers, our suits and dresses, were as human as those of us in the post-industrial world of hedge funds, of insurance, of banking in all its varied forms, who never previously thought of those who died in buildings that collapsed from overloaded floors in ravaging fire and suffocating smoke behind locked fire escapes, or those simply poisoned by the rare metals factories webbed into our innumerable phones and other electronics. We were all human, now. We suspended capital, denied debts and loans, struggled to imagine what the aliens used as matrices for their obviously highly technological society. Some people thought their intervention in our world was proof that capitalism or socialism, that technocracy or theocracy, as practised here or there in lamentably human imperfection, was the answer to how we humans should live. Some people believed that through enlightened reverse engineering we would be able to leap into a future in which there would be no distinction between magic and technology. Some people believed all our typical human problems were soon to be solved. Some people thought this meant that we would now become men like gods. Some people were certain it would only be their like-minded cohorts of religion, of wealth, of skin colour, of nose size, of eye shape who would be selected to gain from untold alien benefits. Some people fled the cities to hide in caves or farms or extensive plantations or private islands or untracked wilderness. Some people abandoned their farms and came to the cities. Some people fanatically insisted on continuing to live no differently than they had before the advent. Some people fatalistically refused to live anything like the way they did before. Some people circulated conspiracy theories. Some people said the aliens were not aliens but actually this or that usual scapegoat, maybe Jewish or maybe Muslim or maybe American. Some people said the aliens were actually artificial intelligence or time travellers or persistent mass hallucinations or a glitch in that endless computer simulation of our human lives. We were wrong.

§

Order this remarkable novel by Michael Kamakana at pulpliterature.com/advent.

FEATURE INTERVIEW

Michael Kamakana

Pulp Literature: *What drew you to writing science fiction in the first place?*

Michael Kamakana: I read SF as a youth — award winners, names like Clarke, Le Guin, Dick, Lem. I admired scientists like my father. I knew I myself would not be a scientist as my interest in math and physics was... time to sleep. I was interested in fantastic escape that I could imagine possible.

PL: *What titles and authors inspired you in the early days?*

MK: *Fountains of Paradise* by Clarke, then *Left Hand of Darkness* by Le Guin, then *The Man in the High Castle* by Dick, then *Neuromancer* by Gibson, then *The Snow Queen* by de Vinge. First non-SF would be *The Great Gatsby* by Fitzgerald, *A Farewell to Arms* by Hemingway, then *Spring Snow* by Mishima, then *In the Labyrinth* by Robbe-Grillet, then *The Name of the Rose* by Eco, then *If on a Winter's Night a Traveller* by Calvino, then *The Woman in the Dunes* by Kobo Abe, then...

PL: *What kind of philosophy books do you read?*

MK: I read almost entirely 'continental' philosophers of the 20th Century. My favourites at the moment are Maurice Merleau-Ponty, Edmund Husserl, Henri Bergson, Gilles Deleuze.

PL: *You and your protagonist both survive a coma. How does your experience with trauma influence your storytelling?*

MK: I always feel that when I truly understand any teaching or experience is when I can write a definitive story inspired by it. For now I keep writing, I keep hoping that someday I will understand the coma.

PL: *You call the stories 'essays.' Why is that? Do you feel that each section is a separate topic?*

MK: Well, the 'reset' and 'reserve' sections came first, and I was inspired by Munif's 'Endings' to use the collective pronouns of 'we' and 'they.' Gradually both collapsing into 'some people', they have generalized, removed, clinical renderings of the times, not much identifiable personal psychology. I think 'essays' could be thought 'fictions' like Jorge Luis Borges.

PL: *You're a prolific writer. Do you work on more than one novel at a time?*

MK: Actually I have about seven works at various stages and interest, with more ideas percolating.

PL: *Did you spend time in Hawai'i as a child? How has this affected the point of view of the narrator of your novel?*

MK: I went to the islands about every winter as a child. We lived on the windward side of Oahu for a year in high school, and Father was working at the University of Hawai'i at Manoa. I still go every February to my mom's hometown, Waimea, on the island of Kaua'i. I can pronounce words in Hawai'ian but cannot converse. I guess I am multicultural as my background is usually one of the first things to learn about me. But I am fortunate that in Canada I look mostly like a dark white guy, whereas in Hawai'i most people recognize me as part Hawai'ian. So, I have never faced much racism here in Canada. I always identified with the 'Indians' in Westerns, with indigenous peoples anywhere. And this work was inspired by reading *Red Gold* by Hemming, which recounts what happened when the Spanish and Portuguese contacted Brazilian indigenes. I just decided to reverse polarities and think of us humans as the technologically primitive and the aliens as the invaders.

Only the start is set in Hawai'i. Most of the essays are not localized as generic North American. The biographical passages are many places. As a beginning, I remember the fear of nuclear war coming to end everything on a beautiful day in Waimea, so this *Advent* is a different end of the world.

PL: *Did you always want to be a writer?*

MK: I knew I was going to be an artist of some sort, only gradually did I realize it was going to be writing. Father's elder sister is an author, Father's younger sister was a visual artist, so this has always been possible, valued, and I suppose reading the first story in my aunt's first collection clarified my desires to do narrative prose. On the other, I have for many years avoided using my family as material because that had upset Father early on in his sister's work.

PL: *Do you have any hopes that Advent will change the way people think about their lives, about aliens, about our many assumptions?*

MK: I hope readers are entertained, are even just momentarily inspired to see themselves and all other humans from an ironic perspective, an existential and historical attitude.

PL: *Did the process of writing* Advent *change the way you felt about yourself as a coma survivor?*

MK: Actually the change developed during the writing: I knew the biographical sections would come down to 'he' then 'I', but only discovered what the aliens want at about the same time I wrote it. I have always had high expectations of myself and limited beliefs in myself, so I am first happy it will be published, then reconciled somewhat to the losses of the coma. Basically, like the aliens decide: I do not know what I would be if not an author.

THE SEVEN SWANS: THE MACHINERIES OF PROGRESS

Mel Anastasiou

When the cogs and wheels of Spencer Stevens's romantic progressions grind to a halt, leave it to the Seven Swans to kick-start things by flinging Spencer back into the early days of the steam railways to solve a mystery that interweaves stolen Saxon gold, perilous deeds, and George Stephenson's Rocket.

Mel Anastasiou is the author of Stella Ryman and the Fairmount Manor Mysteries *(Pulp Literature Press, 2017), longlisted for the Leacock Medal for Humour,* The Extra *(Wooden Bridge Press, 2016), a growing number of novellas featuring Stella Ryman and Spencer Stevens, and several writing guides, including PLP's* The Writer's Boon Companion: Thirty Days Towards an Extraordinary Volume. *You're invited to follow her at melanastasiou.wordpress.com.*

The Seven Swans:
The Machineries of Progress

The Hertfordshire Pub Mysteries in Time, Episode Six, starring Spencer Stevens and the Seven Swans Public House.

Chapter One

Imagine that it's a June morning in Hertfordshire. The trees wave greenly overhead, the canal runs close by the derelict pub you're renovating, and you have fallen headlong in love with a woman whom you've not seen since you and she were twenty. And then imagine that you are a Canadian expat over sixty. And picture this: despite everything they tell you when you're young, age does not cool your hot lover's blood in the slightest. As well, Holly Odell, *née* Wilkerson, is married and lives on the far side of the Pond.

Not sorry for me yet? I wouldn't be, either. For I deserved my hopeless condition. I had managed to arrive at my age broke, alcoholic, and friends with only two beings, *viz.*

1. Byron Standard-Clarke, who had recently run off with my ex-wife Angelica.
2. The Seven Swans, a sixteenth-century public house that

repeatedly slung me back through time to solve mysteries and develop my character and romantic instincts.

I had recently asked Byron for help in my struggle to win back my long-lost love, Holly. Byron gave me a secret, powerful Question. He'd asked this same Question not long ago of my now ex-wife Angelica, and so obtained her affections for himself.

I thought hard before I used Byron's Question because Holly's spouse, Morgan Odell, over there in the States, just might be a good husband. However, her eyes looked sad in her Facebook photos. And although there might be many reasons for unhappiness that had nothing to do with being married to the wrong person, I am not such a good person that I couldn't help hoping she and Morgan were on the rocks. So, I texted her the Question that Byron said moved mountains in a person's life. Here it is:

"What are you going to do, Holly?"

Inside the front door of the Seven Swans Pub, amid the sawdust and gypsum plaster of the ongoing renovations, under a bolt of sunlight from the holey roof, I crouched over my phone and awaited her reply.

I stared at the screen. It stared back. I raised my eyes to the hole in the roof and asked the Seven Swans Pub, "Will this work? Will Byron's question have any effect at all upon Holly?"

The pub didn't answer, of course. But, no sooner were the words out of my mouth than the bit of sky I could see through the hole darkened. Rain teemed down through the roof into the rusty enamelled bath that my good old reno advisors Stan and Eustace had between them hauled into place. I'd said I would tarp the pub's leaky roof in case it rained. I hadn't done it. That was just like me, really. I had created a life much like this pub:

derelict and underfunded. And, maybe loving Holly from afar was enough. Maybe it would have to be. I closed my eyes and listened to the sounds the hearty English weather made upon the un-tarped Seven Swans until at last, mixed in with the splash and clamour of the rain in the metal bath, my phone pinged.

Holly was answering me, all the way from the States.

Here is what she typed in answer to *"What are you going to do, Holly?"* She typed, *"I'm just heading out to weed the garden and sort the recycling. You?"*

This matter-of-fact reply to a Question of power and epic scope threw me for a loop. My thumbs drooped over the screen and then typed as if all on their own, *"No, but I mean, What Are You Going to Do?"*

A long pause followed. Thunder cracked outside. Holly answered, *"What Are YOU Going to Do?"*

Of course, I couldn't explain my actual intentions, which were to free her from Morgan Odell and marry her. So I typed, *"I've got some people coming over the weekend. They're helping me fix up the pub."*

"That's nice of them. Too bad I can't help." She didn't say, too bad *Morgan* and I can't help. My mood brightened somewhat, although the skies above the pub still teemed.

I typed, *"What will you do this weekend?"*

She answered, "*I don't know. Probably argue with Morgan for two days. Have a better weekend than that, Spencer.*"

The rain stopped. I gaped at the phone. The information filled me with wonder. It was true. Her sad eyes had meant exactly what I thought they meant. She wasn't happy with Morgan, and Morgan wasn't happy with her. I stepped outside, did a little dance step on the shining grass, and threw my arms out wide. I said to the Seven Swans Pub, "Miracles can happen."

I gazed at the old pub, built in the Tudor Age and crumbled in the modern one. Stan, Eustace, Cecil, Byron, assorted day labourers, and I had worked hard over the past month. I scanned it for obvious progress and improvement, but the fact was that despite our efforts, the pub looked exactly the same as when I'd arrived here in April. All except the red rose that had grown up by the pub doorway and now had three blossoms that showed clearly against the patched and grubby cream-painted brick exterior.

It was as if renovations had never begun.

I studied the red rose. It had grown a little, if not into the bright-blossomed shrubbery it might someday become. Perhaps the pub would get its roof on and eventually dry out. Perhaps someday I would bring Holly here and walk her through the door into a completed, popular public house.

But she was thousands of miles away. And I had no money to travel to see her. I closed my eyes and imagined myself upon a winged horse, grey as iron, pushing through and over the lowering clouds, rushing me towards Holly.

CHAPTER TWO

1844

The news is out: George Stephenson's train, the famous Rocket, is only minutes away and will soon travel past this very spot, cutting its way through the fields and flowers under a true-blue English sky.

I put off the task the British Museum has set me, that of investigating a possible cache of Saxon gold. The farmer who's rumoured to have dug it up lives just north of here along the shining railway line. If the report of this cache is no hoax, the gold has been here for a thousand years. It will wait, so long as the farmer, named Shooter, doesn't sell the gold before I get there — or let the Roman Britain department, famous for its greed for Roman Britain displays, get there first. If either happens, the head of the Saxon department has sworn that my career at the British Museum will end almost before it begins. But just now, I feel the reckless pull of youth to all that is modern and smart, as George Stephenson and his Rocket call to me with a voice more glamorous than old gold.

The June-hot, Saturday-afternoon crowd mills about, restless and ready to see Stephenson and his great metal beast of an engine, his Rocket. I break from the crowd in the civilized grassy area next to the train tracks in order to follow a group of youngsters to a better view of the excitement.

Children always know where the best spots are for an excellent view. I willingly pay the oldest among them a few coins to lead me among the bushes. This is scratchy work, travelling narrow paths among the blossoming hawthorn and buckthorn. I nearly lose my beaver hat, recently willed to me by an old uncle, when a branch knocks it off my head towards the scrappy boots of my half-grown guides. We emerge closer than I would ever have believed possible to the shiny new tracks, which at this proximity appear wider than their four-and-a-half-foot measure. I set my hat firmly on my head, for I have heard that engines suck, or possibly blow, hot winds that will drag a small animal underneath and crush the poor thing as it passes. I look down at a small boy on my right, trembling with anticipation next to the track. I take hold of the child's dress at the back. He gives me a filthy scowl and pulls himself free. One of my young comrades produces a flat, ovoid bit of copper, and assures us that it was once a penny, placed upon a track. *Broad-gauge track, seven inches wider than this one*, he adds with a tone of engineering authority belied by his grubby ears. We all gaze down at the power-flattened bit of metal. The noise from the crowd on the far side of the shrubbery grows louder.

George Stephenson approaches. Our expert tells us, "The train will arrive from the right, which is south, and travel north."

I hear the train's roar. I taste heat, and the bright metal of its hide. I am filled with excitement so strong that I nearly miss the tug at my hat in my hand. I look down to see the same small boy, still wearing his scowl, trying to take my hat from me. I pull it free of his small fist. I place it on his head. He shows me his two teeth and uses both hands to hold it up so that he can see. I take hold of his skirts again. Stephenson's Rocket is upon us.

The crowd roars outside our hidden viewpoint, and I dare not blink for fear of missing it, for everybody knows that engines travel faster than horses.

Here it comes: first, the chuff of engine breath. And a thrilling, beastly odour so strong that it lifts the hair on my head. I tighten my grip on the skirts of the child at my side. He holds onto the hat.

Now the snub nose appears and next, the gleaming smokestack that dwarfs the tallest beaver hat. Behind the smokestack, the engineer, and at his side none other than George Stephenson. Behind them, the coal car.

I cheer Stephenson and his Rocket, but my voice is lost amid the children's clamouring. The great man holds onto a brass rail by the smokestack. With his other hand he hangs onto his own hat. His face breaks into a grin, and he takes off his hat and waves it. Those of us with hats — including the tiny boy at my side — wave theirs back, and the rest of us stand as tall as possible, even on tiptoe, in hoorah. "Stephenson!"

He is halfway gone, with a rattle of iron wheels on track and the groan of rivets and the squeal of steel against steel, when he addresses us. I shiver with terror that in all the noise I will miss what he says to us. Luckily, he does so at the top of his voice.

I do not miss it.

I hear every letter, every syllable, every space between the words.

He says, loud as a swan's honk and clear as river water, "Children, and you, young sir …" He looks at me, actually at me, as I stand holding tight to the little boy at my side. Now the smokestack is moving into the bushes, out of our sight, but Stephenson is still in view and, thank the heavens above English soil, still talking.

"Huzzah!" the little child cheers, and an older lad says, "Shut your gob and listen."

"Live thunderously," Stephenson says. "And not to outside expectations."

The child cheers again as the engine moves away to our left, out of sight.

"What did he say?" an older lad asks. They all look to me.

I don't answer, for I'm staring at the spot where Stephenson's engine vanished towards the north, and where a smiling young woman, half-hidden around the back of the coal car, her white dress smudged, was waving like a flag that sends off armies. She is a woman where no woman should be. She is a mystery.

CHAPTER THREE

I turn to follow Stephenson's Rocket, and so do the children. The little boy in dresses pulls himself free of me, holding onto my beaver hat so that neither I nor the low-hanging, thorny branches can take it from him.

"Did you see the young woman in the white dress?" I ask the slowest of the group, a ragged youngster with hot green eyes. "Did you see her hanging off the back of the train?"

"Ghosts, here in open country? You're a loon," the youth replies.

I want to work up a riposte, but he's already gone. I'm alone beside the track, without my hat and very dirty on both trouser knees. Shall I chase after my hat, go straight for the Saxon gold, or follow the strange young woman on the back of the train?

Since the dawn of mankind, such a choice has almost made itself.

I follow the train tracks. I walk my way across the shining rails. I shield my eyes from the sun and walk between the rails. Once through the bushes, I reach the crowd that gathered to watch Stephenson pass by. He's gone, but they're still standing here like a lot of cattle, if cattle could talk and laugh as these people do. I balance one boot on each of two rails, raised in height a few inches this way, and scan the onlookers. I can't see the young woman from the train, but I do catch sight of the top of my hat bobbing on the far side of the crowd. I advance towards it with purpose, for if I find the young woman I would rather meet her with my headgear well in place. A fellow my age without a hat looks like an apprentice, and apprentices are notorious for being bad apples and loose company. Of course, I actually am an apprentice, but at the British Museum. We're selected for being sensible good apples, with bright futures in ancient studies.

I advance along the rails, and for the first few steps nobody shows the slightest interest in me.

"Get orff, stupid." It's the boy with the green eyes speaking. The crowd turns and at last takes notice of me.

A cultured voice this time says, "Can't you hear it?"

Another adds, "Attention-seeking hound."

Now that I have their eyes upon me, I feel confident in asking the group at large, "Did anybody here notice a young woman on the back of the train, half-hidden by the coal car?"

I have to raise my voice to continue, for there is a roar approaching. It sounds like thunder, like a train. Above us, skies are clear, but that can change in an instant, given our English weather. I say, "She was wearing a white dress."

"You'll be wearing a shroud an' all," says a young man in shirtsleeves, obviously an apprentice, "if you don't get offen them tracks."

"But ..."

"There's a loop of track not far out, where Stephenson turns the Rocket around," a woman explains.

The train noise roars from the north this time, and heading south. In the nick of time, I leap from the track and dodge the train as it makes its return past us, moving faster than any steed can canter, although slower than a gallop.

My companions from the shrubberies hoot at me and guffaw like ragamuffins at a Punch and Judy show. The smallest boy, wearing my uncle's hat, laughs loudest. I take a step forward, snatch back my hat, and laugh best, for all the gentlemen have their hats in their hands like me, waving back at Stephenson as he passes on his Rocket. All this takes so long that I nearly miss the view of the back of the train. It is empty of hangers-on. The young woman is gone.

I curse silently.

The crowd cheers and moves *ensemble* to follow Stephenson and his Rocket, pushing off to the right to move southwards towards London. I don't know how long they will follow the Rocket — Stephenson is famous for stopping at pubs along the way to take a light lunch and will address the crowd as they stand around his table. The crowd moves right, and I alone move left. I remember that the young fellow said that I might be following a ghost woman.

We who work in the British Museum hear tales of haunts. Some of these ghosts are said to guard Saxon gold and even older treasures left by Romans, Jutes, and other peoples. But we who work in the British Museum don't believe these old tales.

Therefore, the young woman in the white dress exists.

At this thought, I pick up speed. I hurry back onto the train tracks.

I reason that if the girl exists, she travelled northwards towards the loop end of the tracks. If the girl travelled northwards, then she leapt from the train to the north. In which case, she needs no help from me.

Or it might be that she fell.

I speed up my progress, leaping from rail to rail in the direction from which the train travelled.

CHAPTER FOUR

I leap from rail to rail in my second-best boots. The early summer warmth finds its way under the brim of my hat, so that I'm wet behind each ear. I find a rhythm as I work my way along the track, taking two rails at a time, hands in the pockets of my jacket and my tails flying out behind me like a bird's. The soles of my shoes tap out a sharp light song. Words make their way into the rhythm, and they sound something like this: *A modern fellow wants for a modern adventure. A museum man gets sick of the past. But gold*—I jump three rails at once—*is very*—three rails again—*nice indeed.*

Fences woven out of the living hawthorn and buckthorn mark each farmer's boundary. At a small dairy by the tracks, I pay the milkmaid for a cup of buttermilk and slake my thirst before carrying onwards. I keep my eye out for Shooter's farm, which my master at the Museum described as a house with many windows. At the same time, I watch for marks on the ground to show where a girl in a white dress might have fallen or leapt off the train.

I notice some recent marks of violence against the side of a rowan tree trunk, but close observation shows these marks were made by a handsaw, not a fall from the train. I have been walking for a long hot hour under the summer sun looking for the young woman in white, and I still have not reached the spot where Stephenson's standard-gauge track makes its loop. And then I pass among a stand of trees on either side of the track and come out in view of a particular farm.

I know the spot instantly, as I've read the letter that was written by a neighbour of Shooter's and addressed to my master at the Museum. *A house with many windows, a green barn with a red door, and a gazebo to keep the hens in.* You don't see a lot of gazebos these days, since they fell from popularity with the passing of the Hanover kings. Queen Victoria prefers crenellations, when she can get them, and pointy English cone roof toppers. I make a mental vow to return later today, when I hope that my railroad woman mystery will be solved.

I see a white form move inside the gazebo.

I leave the rails to investigate the white shape, and behold, here is the young woman from the coal car, pretending to feed Shooter's chickens. I approach, and she flips her skirt at the hens as if in ignorance of my growing proximity.

When I'm close enough to see that she is about my age, and that her white dress is extraordinarily dirty from the coal car, she gives up her pretence of ignoring me, leaves the hens in the gazebo, and closes the door behind her.

She says, "What are you doing on my father's land?"

I raise an eyebrow, and my hat rises a little with the movement. "Shooter was never your father."

"How would you possibly know, sir? You and I have never met."

"Not formally. But I know perfectly well that no daughter of a Hertfordshire hen-raiser speaks as if through a lemon, like a Bloomsbury scholar."

I smile. She shoos a hen back into the gazebo and turns back to me.

"Again, you are leaping to conclusions," she says. "My mother might have been raised on Russell Street, only to fall in love with the farmer Shooter and run off to marry him. Later, after a falling out, she might have returned with me to London."

"I don't believe a word of it."

"As is your right under British law." She holds out her smudged white skirts in a mock curtsy.

I ask, "Did you fall or jump from Stephenson's train?"

She rolls her eyes. "I jumped. I always jump from trains when I stow aboard them. Your clothing says you're from London, too. Why have you come?"

"Why have *you*?" I parry.

She gestures around her. "I'll give you one of Shooter's chickens as a prize if you guess it."

I look about the dusty but well-kept yard. It is clear from the gazebo that the Shooter family once had money, and from the number of windows overlooking the yard that they enjoy spending money. But the fact that there are chickens roosting in the gazebo speaks to a fall from fortune for the Shooters.

"The first clue," I say, "is that you are here at the same time my master at the British Museum has sent me. You are at the same farm he sent me to, and you had close knowledge of Stephenson's train's route. I therefore surmise ..."

She interrupts me. "Yes, I am a robber, you have guessed it. I am nicely disguised as a well-elevated young woman, but I was actually raised by a master thief in London's cutthroat Seven Dials who has created a secret spy system within the Museum. I am sent to steal the rumoured Saxon gold."

"No, for I would have heard rumours among the other apprentices at the Museum of such a system. Apprentices know every scuttlebutt."

"Well, then, you have found me out. I am myself a master thief, hired by the French government to steal the gold for France."

"Speak some French, then, do."

She meets my challenge with stubborn silence. I am unsurprised.

All educated young ladies such as this one are educated in German and have little or no French beyond common phrases such as *touché*.

I add, "Furthermore, there are no female apprentices at the British Museum, of course, so that leaves family connections, and by elimination of other interested eras, that family connection must be within the Norman Britain department. *J'accuse!*"

She crosses her arms. "I suppose I'll have to give you one of Shooter's chickens now."

"I don't want chickens, but fair play entitles me to truth at the end of a battle."

She scowls. "I am the daughter of the Norman Britain department head. My father is a friend of Stephenson's. I heard them talking at table about the Saxon gold at Shooter's and how it ought to go to the Normans. I made them let me travel up by train to save the day for the Roman Britain department."

"What, alone?"

"I told my father that I would bring my aunt. Look, do you want to steal the gold with me? I only mention it because, with your hat at such an angle, you look capable of anything."

"I am no thief." I sound more apologetic than I mean to. "My master is head of the Saxon department. It's Saxon gold, and we should have it."

"The Normans won over the Saxons in 1066, so why shouldn't they in 1844 as well?"

I set my hat straight on my head. "Ours is clearly a deadly rivalry. My name is Spencer. What is your name?"

"Bellerophon."

"Then, does one call you Belle?"

"One would be sorry."

I look up at Shooter's windows. There is no movement there. I say, "Mind you, the hoard may be a hoax." Bellerophon wants the gold and had to travel by train to get it. I wanted the train and had to search for gold to see it. I'm half in love already. "But the neighbour was convinced the gold was real. My master at the Museum is wary mainly because the fellow is named *Shooter*. My master sent me because I'm quick on my feet. I think the best plan is to ask Shooter suddenly whether he has the treasure, and see whether he flinches in a guilty manner."

"Shooter's gone to Aylesbury," she says. "I heard him speak to a passer-by on the road."

"Did he go on horseback?" I ask. "Or in a wagon?"

"On horseback."

"Interesting," I say. I weigh this information carefully. "Without panniers or any such luggage?"

"Entirely without."

I hold out my hands. "Ergo, the hoard of gold is still here."

"Inside this many-windowed house?"

We regard the house together. I count eleven windows. I picture myself breaking into Shooter's house, and I am suddenly less certain than I was. "If there really is a hoard. The neighbour who reported it might hold a grudge against Shooter."

"There is a hoard," Bellerophon says. "I know it."

"Have you seen it?"

"No, I have felt it. You may have heard that some people feel the tug of gold in their water. It's a gift, like dowsing."

"Do you have the gift?"

"Today I do," she says.

"Ah. Then, let us see whether, working together, Saxon Britain and Norman Britain can get Shooter's kitchen window open."

CHAPTER FIVE

Together we creep inside Shooter's house. We open cupboards, lift floorboards, and move blankets and cushions aside. We find nothing but mouse nests and tobacco ash. We return to the yard and walk its breadth and width, searching for soft ground in which to bury gold, but the yard is all hard packed. I crawl under the gazebo while the hens look on as if I am the most interesting sight they have seen. The earth is packed so hard under here that scraps of chicken feed lie atop the earth like scarab dung.

Two people who know what they are looking for can soon exhaust all possible hiding places for a large treasure, even in an untidy farmhouse and largish yard. Bellerophon and I stand side by side, gazing about at the buildings and the tall lines of shrubbery out by the road.

She asks, "He wouldn't have hidden the gold back where he found it?"

"And have somebody see him do it? And dig it up for their own? Unlikely."

"Might he not have divided it up among his friends, and they are hiding it for him?"

"It's not possible for a number of men to keep such a secret while there are public houses with strong ale sold in them."

She nods.

We both gaze across the hard-packed farmyard to Shooter's fence and the recently laid track. The sun is setting, and the track is in shadow now.

Bellerophon says, "This was quite a Saturday."

I nod. "I saw George Stephenson." And met Bellerophon.

She says, "You'll see him tomorrow as well, for he rides out Sundays. I plan to ride back with him. With the gold."

Night falls. I suggest heading into town for a bite to eat and rooms for the night. Bellerophon insists on concealing ourselves underneath the gazebo. "He will check for his gold when he comes back," she says. "And we know that it's not hidden inside."

"And if he does not?"

"He will at least look in the hoard's direction. He won't be able to help himself."

I know how he feels. I take off my hat and we crawl under the gazebo to wait for Shooter to come home. The hens, out of support for our British cause, or because they grow bored with looking at us under the gazebo, go quietly to roost, and we are alone. I set my hat down beside my head. Presently, we sleep. Or rather, I drift and Bellerophon sleeps.

I keep myself awake by imagining the Saxon treasure on display for generations to come, in a hundred years, perhaps, when trains will travel faster than the wind. I pinch myself and do not fall asleep.

But somehow it is morning, and the chickens are making a racket around the perimeter of the gazebo. Is Shooter home? I peer out to see that the yard beyond the gazebo's perimeter is brightly lit.

Shooter's horse is tied up near his kitchen door. The day is here.

Bellerophon is not.

CHAPTER SIX

Shooter is back at his farm. He must have betrayed his treasure's hiding place somehow to my companion beneath the gazebo — with a look, or perhaps with a visit to the hoard, just as Bellerophon anticipated he would. And now she has gone out to find the treasure.

I remember her soft scholar's hands. It will take her a long time to dig up the gold. I remember her hard head and conclude that she will not stop until she has it.

Shooter's house has many windows, and he is bound to see her. Perhaps he has seen her already.

I leave my hat and hurry out from under the gazebo to stand in the yard among the chattering chickens. It takes me only a moment to spy Bellerophon, crouching on the train track, the rails. She has a stick in one hand and she is digging at the soil there.

I run towards her, dodging chickens underfoot. To one side a window opens wide in Shooter's house. I shout at her to move off the track. She scowls and shakes her head. Shooter will have seen us both.

I hear the noise of Stephenson's train, approaching on its Sunday ride.

I rush towards her.

Shooter bangs out his door and heads towards us, looking strong and quick as a bull.

Stephenson's train approaches on the far side of the greenery.

I don't know that he will see her there. Her dress is white and catches the morning sun. But I remember the smokestack out front that may well block her from view. And there is nobody here but me to stop it.

If I run to stop the train, I will be leaving her to Shooter's mercies.

I can't stop Shooter, because the train is about to run down Bellerophon.

I reach her and pull at her to stop digging and get off the track. "The train is coming."

"Stephenson is a gentleman and won't hit me with it. And, I need proof of the treasure before Shooter stops me," she calls, and digs harder.

She pulls it from me and continues to dig. Shooter is halfway to the rails.

The noise of the train increases.

"Dig, before Shooter can stop us," she says. "I will have the credit. Or you will."

I say, "We will share it, for we will both be dead."

"We will pull free in time."

Bellerophon's hands, soft and white, dig quickly in search of treasure. She pushes aside the summer-dry soil. I see in her movements the same fevered haste that the original Saxons must have felt, keeping treasure safe from invaders. Now I stand over her in much the same position a Saxon warrior might take up to guard her from the coming armies. The Saxons might have saved some of their gold, but they couldn't halt the Normans from taking over their world. The train, with all its promise of progress, its gnashing wheels, its hissing steam, is at least as unstoppable as they were.

She pulls from the soil a dusty golden torc. I find a ring set with a mottled red stone and pull it free.

"That should be enough even for you. Get off this track."

"My skirt is caught," she says.

"Tear it," I say. Together we attempt pull it free.

A voice barks, "That's my chalcedony."

I turn at the cry.

It is Shooter, arrived at the rails. "The treasure was on my land, and it is mine."

"Queen Victoria will have it," I tell him sternly. "And the British Museum."

I stand between Bellerophon and the invisibly approaching train.

Still pulling at her skirt, I tell Shooter, "I can't leave Bellerophon. Will you please stop this train?"

"Yes, please do," Bellerophon says, still holding the torc in one hand while she tugs at her skirt.

"Anyway, you might as well be a hero as a villain," I add. "Either way, you won't get the gold."

The noise from the approaching train is stupendous. It makes me think of cannons roaring and Nelson's hero's death at sea, never forgotten by the British peoples nor likely to be.

The train steams out of the greenery.

Shooter swears and runs past us, signalling to Stephenson and the engineer. There is a hiss that sounds like a million swans, and the train eases to a stop not far from us.

Stephenson and his engineer climb down from the train and let us all know how relieved they are to see that we are safe.

I claim the gold for the British Museum.

Stephenson cheers and tells us that we all could use a cup of something strong. Shooter brings out a jug of ale from his pantry. We all toast the Saxon gold and the hero Shooter. He vows to dig up the rest of the gold this very day and cart it all down to the British Museum. Stephenson and his engineer promise not to run him down with the train while he digs, and in fact the engineer stays with Shooter in order to join him with a coal shovel. George Stephenson elects to stay as well, to cheer them on. Bellerophon and I watch to make sure Shooter doesn't pocket any of it.

So, when the day's work is done, Shooter's cart and horse are brought forward to be loaded with coins, plate, cups, chains, and one chalcedony-set ring. I disguise the treasure with an old blanket. I retrieve my hat from under the gazebo. I fold myself into the back of the cart for the trip to London with my boots tucked under me. I charge myself with guarding the hoard from any possible robbers, and even more from Shooter changing his mind about the heavy cost in Saxon gold of being a hero.

Bellerophon joins George Stephenson on the train, and they chug off and around the loop a little farther north. I hear the cheer of a waiting crowd not far off from Shooter's farm. By the time I am well settled in the cart and Shooter has his carthorse watered and ready, the train returns, heading southwards. The Rocket picks up speed and crosses the dug-up spot underneath the track where the treasure was buried.

Bellerophon, grubbier than ever, stands beside George Stephenson, behind the smokestack. She waves to Shooter and me as they pass. I know she will be first back with the news, and her father will gain credit by this for the Norman Britain Department, rather than my own master in the Saxon Department. But I know in my heart that it is the British Museum, and the British people we serve there, who are the winners this day.

And among them, a loyal subject: myself. I take off my hat to Bellerophon. Her dress flaps like a flag of victory held high by the Normans as they entered Britain.

The train is a much finer way to travel than the rear of Shooter's cart, jostled and folded like the old blanket that hides the gold. Who among us lives thunderously? It seems to me that, the glories of progress aside, all forms of transport get a person to the place he wants to go and to whom he wishes to call upon, should she be amenable to callers.

CHAPTER SEVEN

I opened my eyes to see a Virgin train disappearing among the rowans, heading towards London at a speed not just greater than a horse could run, but many times that.

Live thunderously.

Stephenson's words still echoed in my head. Despite my

financial circumstances, my age, and my indecision, I wanted exactly that: to live thunderously. But was there anything less thunderous than my life as it stood?

I wanted to be like that train, bellowing my way across the miles to Holly. Instead, I was more like my cellphone: I communicated but went nowhere.

Well, then, maybe I could write Holly a poem. A poem would, in fact, be the perfect action for an inactive fellow like myself. I could write a bold and thunderous poem to Holly.

I stared up at the Seven Swans. Stan's ladders were stacked neatly towards the back of the pub. There Eustace had straightened and wiped clean paint pots, tidied tool boxes, wound up cords, and covered anything that could be harmed by rain or sun with tarpaulins. I admired the organizational powers of Stan and Eustace, and the way they got things done. They didn't let their eighties stop them doing what they felt inspired to do. I couldn't let my sixties stop me. I would climb up a ladder, balance on the rooftop of the Seven Swans, and declaim my poem to Holly, once I had written it.

I struggled to think up a first line. It was hard going, for the name *Holly* immediately called up second-line rhymes *jolly, wally, and collie.*

Stan and Eustace appeared around the corner of the Seven Swans. They were heading my way, wearing the happy and confident expressions of men who had accomplished much already this day and had earned their morning pint of Guinness.

I said, "How's it going, fellows?"

"Like British Rail, my lad," Stan said. "Slow and arsey."

"Don't say that where George Stephenson can hear you," I murmured.

"Don't worry yourself, though." Stan gazed up at the pub and its leaky roof. "It may not be visible to the untutored eye, but there are changes happening in the revered Seven Swans."

"Plumbing." Eustace tapped the side of his nose with an index finger.

Stan nodded. "It's the heart and soul of a building, my old son."

"Proper pipework establishes strength of character," Eustace clarified.

Byron followed them out from behind the pub. The sunshine lit his yellow cashmere pullover. He swung a hammer in one hand as if it were a tennis racquet and he were warming up for singles at Wimbledon.

"We're off to the Lamb for a pint," he announced.

"Drink in good health," I said.

They all three exchanged glances, and there was a certain amount of shifting of feet. Everybody always appeared uncomfortable around my alcoholism, especially when they were going for a drink.

"It's completely fine with me if you head off to the Lamb," I said.

Eustace nodded approvingly. "Good company is better than drink."

"I wish you could come with us," Stan said. "There's nothing better at the end of a day than a good stiff drink."

Byron said, "Yes, that's how Spencer got to be an alcoholic in the first place."

"Not anymore," Eustace said. "Spencer is a lesson to us all in the benefits of moderation."

I said, "That's very kind of you. But I won't come with you. I have something to work out."

Byron straightened his collar. "I read somewhere that they're doing wonders with non-alcoholic beer these days."

"Really, that's not why I'm staying behind," I insisted. "You three go on ahead. I'll follow in a little while and stand you all a round of cheese and onion crisps."

They peered closely at me. Stan put his small, beefy hand on my shoulder and led me to the front of the Seven Swans, where it was closest to the canal. A rickety picnic table leaned a little drunkenly towards the pub. Stan sat me down. "You rest, now. These two always forget that you're not in the first bloom of youth. Younger men than you have popped their clogs through overwork. Mark my words."

I leaned my head on my hands and shut my eyes. "I'll be along in a minute."

I heard them shuffle away.

There followed a long moment of silence, and then the click of metal on wood. I opened my eyes.

Byron, alone with me now, had set the hammer down onto the table. "Spencer, old man, you're a mystery wrapped in an enigma today, and it's a great irritation to me."

I decided that nothing would come of writing a poem to Holly except the thrill of disclosure, like whispering secrets in an empty room. It seemed to me that this was not a bad way of describing cowardice.

I said, "Byron, I need you to get me some money."

"For cheese and onion flavoured crisps?" His tone was lazy, but his gaze was sharp. "Or airfare?"

For now, I'd keep my plans to myself.

"I want to pay Stan and Eustace a better per-hour rate." As soon as I said it, I knew this was true.

"What, are you offering respect and proper payment for our

elders? What a good idea. I owe those two codgers a break. They always make me feel quite youthful."

"Thanks." I stood up. A train was approaching, heading south towards London. I didn't know how yet, but I would follow it soon. All praise the machineries of progress. They made the world smaller, as small as would seem to a man with seven-league boots striding from hill to valley, hopping over rivers, all the way to the true blue Atlantic Ocean and beyond.

§

The seventh and final episode of **The Hertfordshire Pub Mysteries in Time**, *featuring Spencer Stevens and the Seven Swans Public House, will appear in* Pulp Literature Issue 21, *Winter* 2019.

FIRST DATE

Maria Pascualy

Maria Pascualy lives in Tacoma, Washington, where she writes in a little white house. Her writing has appeared in Panoply, Mulberry Fork Review, and Hobo Camp Review.

First Date

Her sleek ginger beard slid between her breasts
as they talked about the weather.
She had baby cow eyes, brown and deep
& baby cow lashes, pink at the tips.

He brushed her elegant wrist with his hook.
I was going to order the lobster bisque.
She nodded in agreement. Would it drip?
Her hands at rest were milky white

& smooth as shucked oysters.
She moved the rosebud in the small cut-glass vase
an inch closer to his bread plate.
She used the same pink lacquered fingernail

to etch a spiral in the starched white napkin.
I'm having a very nice time. She picked up her glass
of red wine & looked in his eyes.
A sliver of light cut through the curtain

First Date

& bounced round the curve of his silver hook.
A tiny green lizard, the size of a gumdrop,
cut across the white tablecloth
then stood on its back feet, waiting, at attention.

THE SLADE TRANSMUTATION

Richard J. O'Brien

Richard *lives in New Jersey where he teaches writing and literature at Rowan College at Gloucester County and Stockton University. His novels include* The Garden of Fragile Things, Infestation, *and* Under the Bronze Moon. *Visit Richard at obrienwriter.com and follow him @obrienwriter on Twitter.*

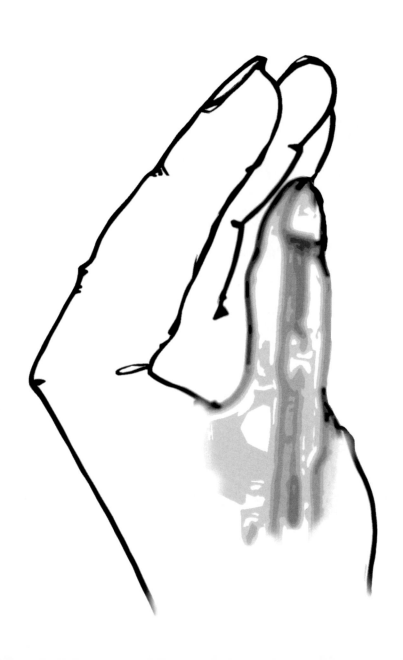

The Slade Transmutation

One winter morning I woke up with a titanium alloy toe. It was still dark when my alarm clock went off. When it came to moving around in the dark, I was the worst. I could not get from my bed to the bathroom without stubbing a toe on something—the bed frame, the dresser, the nightstand, it didn't matter. If it was in the room and a solid object, chances were I came into contact with it in a hard way.

My wife Katie was still asleep. When the alarm clock sounded I shut it off quickly and got out of bed. Katie stirred as I made my way toward the bathroom. My left foot connected with the chair in front of Katie's make-up table. A clanking noise sounded but I felt no pain. The chair tipped over and fell on its side.

"What are you doing?" Katie asked.

She turned on the lamp on her nightstand.

The chair leg that I had kicked was splintered at the bottom, as if someone had taken an axe to it. I stood the chair upright and let it go. The chair toppled over again.

"I broke it," I said.

"Jack, you didn't," said Katie.

The chair leg I had kicked was a full inch shorter than the other three now. That was the first time I noticed the little toe on my left foot that shone in the pale light against the blue carpet. I flicked the little toe with my finger. It rang like a small bell.

"What was that?" Katie asked.

"My little toe," I told her.

"Are you kidding me?"

"See for yourself."

I walked around the bed and lifted my foot.

Katie could not believe it. I didn't either. Neither of us knew that morning that the little toe was the just the start of it.

Dr Billings looked perplexed. He had been our family doctor for several years. Tall, thin, his long white hair pulled back in a perpetual pony tail, he did little to mask his surprise.

"It looks like an alloy," he said. Then he tapped it with a pen. "Does that hurt?"

"I can't feel a thing," I told him.

Katie stood in the corner of the examination room, chewing on her fingernails the way she always did whenever she encountered bad news. That problem that afternoon was that no news had been delivered yet. My wife was already getting a head start.

"You want to get it removed?" asked Dr Billings.

Katie drew in an audible breath.

"No," I said. "Then I'd be down to nine toes."

"You work in construction?" he asked.

"Roofing and siding mostly these days," I said. "Work's scarce."

"I'd like you to go over to the university hospital," Dr Billings said. "Let them have a look at it."

"To what end?" Katie asked.

"Have you experienced any lost time recently?" the doctor asked, ignoring my wife's question.

"Is this a joke?" I asked. "What are you implying? Aliens?"

"I am just trying to figure out who could graft this thing on you with such precision," Dr Billings said. "It really is top-notch work."

"Does our government have anything like this?" I asked.

"Oh, God," Katie moaned.

"What?"

"I should have never let you watch all those shows about abductions," she said.

"You'll need X-rays," said Dr Billings. "I can give you a referral."

"Thanks," I said. "And doctor?"

"Yes?"

"Let's not discuss this with anyone else," I said. "I am ... that is, my wife and I are already freaked out enough."

"Carol will give you a referral slip," he said. "I will request copies of the X-rays. Carol will set you up with a follow-up appointment."

At the receptionist's desk Carol handed me a referral slip. Then she dropped the bad news.

"The doctor's booked up solid for the next three weeks," said Carol the receptionist. "I'll put you down for today a month from now?"

"Fine," I said.

My wife said nothing as we walked out to my pick-up truck. Before we left, I took hold of her and hugged her close.

"I don't understand any of this," she sobbed.

"Then that's two of us," I said.

The following morning I woke up and turned off the alarm clock. When I did, the damn thing collapsed into a pile of plastic and circuit boards, producing a limited display of sparks.

"What now?" Katie cried.

"I crushed my alarm clock with my finger," I told her.

"Very funny."

"I'm serious. Just listen."

My left index finger matched my little toe. I tapped it against the night stand. A different tone sounded: a distant gong.

I swung my legs off the bed. As soon as I did I wished that I had not. My other nine toes matched my little toe on my left foot and my left index finger. When I flicked my new finger against my new toes there was no hollow ringing. I tapped my index finger against the night stand again. Like my toes, it sounded more solid already.

Katie left me no choice but to go to the university hospital. It was all the way in the city, at least an hour away, and I hated that commute. I wanted to wait another day or two and see what might come next. My wife had other ideas.

No sooner had we checked into the hospital I was met with a small cadre of doctors and specialists like I was some kind of medical anomaly. In the mix, Katie was shown to a waiting area by four nurses who did everything they could to assure my hysterical wife that everything would be fine.

One of the specialists was named Dr Radha Singh. He was a short guy with a ridiculous moustache that reminded me of old-time baseball players. He walked into the examination room humming 'Follow the Yellow Brick Road', and I knew instantly that I liked him.

"So," said Dr Radha, "you are turning into metal, yes?"

"Maybe you can tell me," I said.

"If I was a betting man," he said, "I would say it's titanium alloy."

"What makes you say that?"

"I don't know for sure. It just looks like the same material used to make surgical instruments. Very durable. It's used for many things. Tanks, bicycles, oil rigs. You name it."

"That's great, but what do I do now?"

Dr Singh fiddled with his moustache.

The plan was for me to remain at the hospital to do tests. I told Dr Singh I had to consult with my wife.

Katie and I ducked into an elevator and rode down to the first floor. We made it out of the hospital without incident. It wasn't every day that a patient sought help for appendages being replaced by titanium alloy parts. Or maybe it was, since none of the staff at the university hospital seemed to care that we left.

That night I barely slept. In the morning, my new alarm clock went off. Katie was feeling extra amorous. She draped her arm across me and nuzzled close.

"Jesus Christ," she muttered and tapped on the side of my face with her knuckle.

I got out of bed and went to the mirror on the closet door. In the dark I could see something was wrong. When Katie turned on the light it only exacerbated the situation.

A good portion of the right side of my face was gone, replaced by the still-unfamiliar titanium alloy. The new part extended from just above the eyebrow, over my nose, across my cheek, and back to where my right ear should have been. There was no right eye to speak of either; when I covered my left eye, my human eye, I could still see.

Katie turned on the nightstand lamp on my side of the bed.

I raised my left hand to touch the satin-finish alloy on the right side of my face. Until that moment I had no idea that my entire left hand, and a good portion of my forearm, had been replaced.

"You can't go to work like that," she said.

My wife climbed off the bed, a little unsteady on her feet when she reached the floor, and came to my side.

Someone banged on the front door as they rang the doorbell over and over again.

It turned out Katie was right. I would not be going to work that day.

The government was at my front door.

Some idiot played Saga's 'On the Loose' at top volume on a continuous loop while they kept the lights on in my secured room. I hadn't heard that song since the early 1980s, and by my estimation I had not slept in nearly five days. Even now, I am not sure which experience was worse.

When they came for me that morning there wasn't much use putting up a fight. For one, there were too many of them. At least they had the common decency to allow Katie to visit me every day. The hours of visitation, however, were another matter. They changed them every day. Worse, even Katie didn't know where they were keeping me, since she was brought to the facility blindfolded and made to wear sound-cancelling earphones that played 80s industrial music.

Katie had hated New Order and Depeche Mode when we were young. She had flirted with the notion of becoming a Deadhead, but in truth she was too much of a germ freak to ever completely immerse herself in the lifestyle. Me? I didn't care much for the Grateful Dead. Or New Order and Depeche Mode, for that matter. Anyway, Katie was allowed ninety minutes with me, always before dark and never at the same hour of the day.

"Are you sleeping?" she asked.

My wife already knew the truth. Though she would be hard-pressed to tell, since my human eyes were gone by the third day and sixty percent of my body was composed of titanium alloy. During one of her visits, Katie leaned her head against the chassis that had once been my chest.

"No physical contact, please," a voice said over a speaker in the visitation room.

"When are they going to let you out of here?" she asked.

"Hard to say," I told her.

"Your voice sounds strange, Jack."

"It is synthetic," I replied.

"That's not funny."

"It's true."

As near as I could tell, my neck and head had been replaced by robotic features. My voice sounded like I was speaking through a Moog synthesizer. And since I didn't have any eyes to speak of, at least not what Katie was used to, it stood to reason that my brain had been replaced by something else. This much a neurosurgeon among my captors had already hypothesized. Without cutting through my alloy head, there was no way of knowing for sure. It wasn't like they hadn't tried already. Diamond-tipped drill bits and saw blades, lasers: nothing worked.

A little more than a week had passed since I'd woken up with a new toe. Now better than half my body had been mysteriously replaced with what the goons who held me prisoner couldn't decide were robotic parts or some alien-android upgrade.

"Why is it always the same music?" Katie asked.

"I suppose they think it annoys me," I answered.

"It doesn't?"

"There are worse bands than Saga."

A bell rang outside the room. That meant the visit was over.

Katie stood up and hugged me. We were not permitted physical contact, but neither of us cared. It was over in an instant.

"I was just thinking," she said as she waited for one of the guards to unlock the door. "Why are you still wearing clothes?"

When Katie wasn't there, time slowed down. I didn't put up much of a fight when they cut small holes in my flesh to insert fibre-optic cameras. They let me watch as the camera neared some area inside my body that was no longer human. Whenever the camera got close to the robot part of me, the image on the display screen went blank.

"Are you doing that?" one of my examiners asked every time it happened.

"No," I said.

"Maybe if we insert the fibre-optic camera first," another doctor said. "And then turned it on."

A sneak attack. Brilliant.

These guys, I assumed, had gone to decent medical schools and had jumped through innumerable bureaucratic hoops just to get the clearance to work in a secret facility. Now, as they faced the inevitability of not finding an answer of what was happening to me, they bickered like children on a playground. The window for further internal exploration was getting smaller. And they knew it.

"**Why** do you keep the lights on?" I asked one night.

The guard pointed to the cameras in each corner of the room where I slept.

"They want to see if some non-local entity is responsible," he replied.

"You mean like from a parallel universe?"

"Mr Slade," said the guard, "I'm not really at liberty to say."

"Why not?"

"I shouldn't be talking to you."

"Imagine a whole army of me."

"I'd rather not."

"How's that? I am sure you don't get into your position by sending off for a security guard certificate in the back of a comic book."

"Mr Slade?"

Clearly, the guard was too young to know what I was talking about. Another child of the digital age.

"Never mind," I said. "What's happening to me could be happening in other places. Did you guys hear anything in the ether?"

"Ether?"

"You know. Chatter?"

"I am not at liberty to say."

"It might be cool to have an army like me."

The guard relaxed somewhat. Then he offered, "I heard they can't cut through you."

"Not yet. Hey, are you thinking what I am thinking?"

"Mr Slade." The guard placed his right hand over his sidearm. "I am not going to shoot you."

"Try it."

"I might kill you."

"Maybe," I said. "Or maybe I'm turning into Superman. Or Iron Man. You know what I mean."

The guard's relief came some time later. I didn't bother the midnight-to-eight man. He was a real tool.

My wife didn't show up one day. Or the next. Or the one after that.

"A situation like this can prove to be stressful," said one of the doctors.

They wouldn't let me use a phone. And although they claimed to send someone out to fetch my wife, I wasn't sure I believed them.

Katie's making herself scarce for a visit was the least of my troubles that day. The doctor who had told me about stress was the one who broke the bad news.

No part of me was human now.

Sleep was no longer an issue. I didn't need it.

After hearing that Saga song for the three thousandth time since they took me prisoner I decided I had had enough. I still didn't know if I was bulletproof, or grenade-proof for that matter, but I decided I wanted out.

The midnight-to-eight man arrived the way he always did. He never said a word to me.

"Hey," I said. "What do you get when you cross an omelette with a kangaroo?"

Nothing. He was one icy bastard.

"Okay." I switched gears now. "A rabbi, a priest, a circus clown, and an accountant walk into a strip bar. The dancer on stage is this gal wearing a Wookie mask. So the priest says ... wait. You do you know what a Wookie is, right?"

The ice man kept on staring straight ahead. He was dressed like the other guards. Black khakis, a ridiculous beret, a bullet-proof vest, and combat boots. He wore a semi-automatic pistol in a holster on his waist along with what were either smoke bombs or grenades. I just had to find out.

Wouldn't you know it? They turned out to be grenades. After the first grenade went off, the midnight-to-eight man was already dead. I detonated the second grenade as well, and I didn't feel a thing, not even the concussive waves that took the door off its hinges.

After that, it was like a security guard reunion. At least until I killed them all. Once I took out the security force all the egghead doctors went running off into the night.

The strange thing is I never found where they were playing Saga's 'On the Loose', and believe me, after hearing it a few thousand times I wanted nothing more than to find the room where the music player was located and smash it to bits. Robbed of such vengeance, I left the facility, which turned out to be some forgotten brick building with no windows on the ass-end of Fort Dix, New Jersey.

It was already dark out by the time I got home. Katie was there, but she wasn't alone. There were six mercenary-looking types in those familiar black uniforms along with some guys in suits.

"Leave now," I said. "And I will forget this whole thing."

"Take her," one of the suits said.

The goon closest to Katie unholstered his pistol and held it to my wife's head. So I killed the others just to level the playing field.

"I'll kill her," the uniformed goon said. "I swear to God."

Katie was wearing white gloves. It was warm out. So the gloves didn't make any sense at all.

"Just walk away," I told the government goon.

The moment I spoke, Katie reached up, took hold of the pistol's barrel, and bent it. The goon attempted to pull the trigger but the pistol no longer worked. In an instant he produced a knife from the back of his belt.

Katie jabbed her gloved right hand into the guy's left eye. When she pulled her hand away the glove remained inside the gaping wound she had created in the guy's face. The goon dropped to his knees and slumped over on his back.

Katie held up her ungloved hand. It looked like mine, titanium alloy with a satin finish. She took off the other glove to show me the three metallic fingers on that hand. Next, she kicked off her right shoe. Her foot was no longer human. Suddenly, a thin sliver of alloy showed on her left cheek and spread down her neck.

My wife never looked more beautiful.

MY BROTHER PAULIE: A DOMESTIC SPACE ODYSSEY

Alex Reece Abbott

Alex's *short fiction has been selected for many collections, including* Bonsai: The Big Book of Small Stories, Dusk, *Word Factory's* Citizen: The New Story, The Broken Spiral, *and* Heron. *She has won the Northern Crime Competition, the Crediton, Arvon, and HG Wells Grand Prizes, and often places and shortlists. Alex's literary historical novel,* The Helpmeet, *was a winner in the 2016 Greenbean Irish Novel Fair. 'My Brother Paulie: A Domestic Space Odyssey' was developed during a workshop with award-winning writer and diversity campaigner Kit de Waal, and was shortlisted for* Pulp Literature's *2017 Raven Short Story Contest. Alex's website is alexreeceabbott.info.*

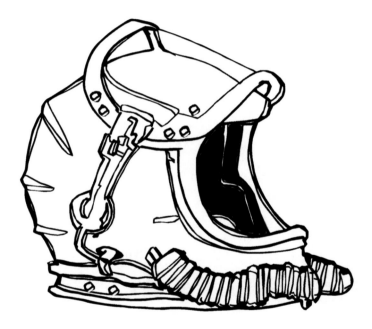

MY BROTHER PAULIE:
A DOMESTIC SPACE ODYSSEY

Docking

"Hey, Major Tom. Lunch? Baked beans . . ."

Paulie stares through me.

Can't blame him, it's hardly the fare of space travellers.

"Fancy docking for a shower?"

What's caused his latest lift-off? Like space exploration, medicine is an inexact science.

Mostly, we never find out.

Deep Space

Everyone has an opinion about my brother Paulie, but I'll tell you something. From before.

He loved space as a boy. Apollo, Sputnik. Rockets. Asteroids. Planets.

Now he's on a voyage of discovery from my most comfortable armchair.

His spacesuit — a knitted, cyclamen-pink onesie — covers him, apart from a small oval visor, like our snorkelling masks when we were kids.

But Paulie's twenty-three and he's not coming up for air.

Exploration

By day three, stifling wet-dog wafts of old wool and stale sweat are rising.

"Even aliens wash their clothes and brush their teeth," I say, although I have no evidence.

In his galaxy, he lines up his meds just like he arranged the space rocks he'd gather from our backyard. And, he rocks. Fro and to.

Uncontactable in the vacuum of space.

Eclipsed.

I wait and watch for his re-entry.

Somewhere in his head, there's been a control failure.

Re-entry

When they came for Paulie, he explained about his spacesuit malfunction.

After the shot, he went with them to get a new suit. Didn't struggle much.

Safe landing, I called.

His space rocks are lined up on my coffee table.

I've tried incense, even essential oils. That smell might be permanent.

ORDINARY

Sylvia Stopforth

Sylvia Stopforth *is a university archivist. Her stories, essays, and poems have appeared in* Room, The New Quarterly, [spaces], *and* Shy (University of Alberta Press). *For more than ten years she has served as a regular (but not necessarily ordinary) column editor for* BC History *magazine. Her short fable 'Dragon Rock' was turned into a sequential art story by Mel Anastasiou for the Summer 2014 issue of* Pulp Literature, *and we're delighted to bring you a longer prose piece from her this summer.*

ORDINARY

When I am born, my parents, they do not celebrate. I am a girl, after all. And they are new to this country and feel it would be unseemly. Tempting the fates. Most of the wild ones, the feyen, they do not care. My parents are poor. The feast would have been sorely lacking and the musicians of lower quality.

But the Old One, she takes offense.

After the sun goes down she comes, unbidden. And she will give a gift. My parents implore. They know the stories. Girls who fall into a sleep like death. Others who must live their lives with foxes' ears, or hiding tails beneath their skirts. But she does not heed them. I imagine their words are like the whine of insects in her ears. They tell me she is a fearsome thing with tiny, sharp bones through her ears and 'round her throat, threaded there like a necklace. Her eyes are heavy-lidded, her hair shorn beneath a coronet of uncut, dully glittering stones. She is dressed all in black. In my mind her cloak of crows' wings glistens like the elytra of the darkling beetle. She stretches out her hand. My mother, ever fastidious, sees that there is dirt beneath the broken nails.

The child, she says, will be wholly ordinary.

And they do not know. Is this a curse? Or a blessing?

For my part, I know. I know exactly.

The other villagers, they tell me I fuss about nothing. That being ordinary is no great misfortune. On the contrary, they say, being outside of ordinary is the true encumbrance. They bleat about the burden of possibility.

Their words are like the whine of insects in my ears.

I hold a knife in my hand … or is it a sharpened bone? To cut it out of them, this gift they do not want.

I am eight when it begins to matter, when I know that something is wrong. The other children are petted and praised when they do something particularly pleasing, and smacked when they misbehave. I am smacked, to be sure, but only when my mother is angry with everything and nothing satisfies her. For my own actions, for my own self, there is neither praise nor punishment.

If I am sent to fetch a bucket of water, I will do it. I will not bring back two, shoulders fiery with pain, as Bran does, like a dog that rolls over to show its soft belly when the larger dogs come too close. But neither do I see that any gain comes from evading work or grumbling about it. I am not quick, nor do I lag behind. I am neither especially kind nor given to cruelty. I am common, middling. As ordinary as a housefly.

Oh, there is a time when I try for the quick, pleased smile from my mother, the softening of my father's voice. I clean my father's pipe for him, without being asked. But the bowl cracks. There was already a fine fissure working its way across, but he does not remember this, and I am beaten and sent to bed without supper.

Then Esla comes. It is a difficult birth, and the baby has the colic, so I take care of Fartha and Bran, warming their oatmeal and scrubbing their faces and hands. There is a teacher that year, so I help Bran with his new shoes. On the way to school he trips and breaks his nose. For my efforts, I am granted another beating, though my father knows full well the shoes are too large. He will grow into them, my mother says, when she buys them from the tanner's wife.

There is a teacher again when I am twelve. This one says the girls must also learn. I like school. It is like turning over a rotting log to see all the scurrying, scuttling creatures beneath. Best of all is reading. I can already read the clouds, and the stars, and the passage of an animal in the undergrowth. Now I also read letters and words. It is satisfying. Exact and exacting. The teacher says I have a knack, but while he speaks his eyes linger on Fartha. I do not care. I know she is beautiful and I am not. And it does not matter because at last I have found something the Old One cannot poison.

I spend hours at my lessons. If I am not working or sleeping, I am reading or scratching letters into bark with the dull blade of an old knife. I resolve not to draw any attention to myself. I miss words deliberately. The teacher barks, disappointed, and I sit down. I rest my head on my arms. They think I hide my shame, but it is because I cannot keep the smile from my lips. Is it possible I am better than the others at something?

But then it slips sideways. There is a sharp band of pain around my head when I try to read. In school, the letters on the slate swim. I move closer, I squint, but I cannot make them still. My mother finds me crying in the lean-to over the pig slop and tells my father I must stop going to school. Clearly it is too much for me, and I am making myself ill. I only cry harder at this, but she is deaf to my words. I beg, I storm, I scream. Never before have I wanted something so much. I am beaten and sent to bed without supper.

Around the time the black flies hatch, the teacher falls ill with a fever. After only a few days he is dead. It is as if someone has taken him away. There is not another teacher from that day to this.

So there is only one possibility left to me. Do I dare? The prospect fills me with fear, but also with something else. Something that makes my heart thrum in my ears.

I begin with a small intention. I leave the door of the hen house open, whisper-call the lurking stoat. But the birds are charmed. No harm befalls them.

Esla brings me a furred orange and black worm curled up tightly in her palm. It is a moth, before it is a moth. She has rescued it from the side of the lane where Tunny's fields lie open to the blue sky. There is a strong scent of smoke in her hair. When the leaves turn, Tunny burns off the spent stalks and grasses. He says it is cleansing, and flushes the vermin from their hidey-holes. But the soil does not require cleansing, surely. It is made for life. And the burrowing things, the gnawing things, the small, secret things, they are a part of that life.

Night falls, and everyone sleeps. It is not so dark. The moon is near full, winking in and out of the scudding clouds. But it is cold. I slip the latches, open stall doors. The horses' muzzles are soft against my hands. The hay catches easily, and hungry tongues lick the doorframe. I turn and run, and the horses, frightened now, scatter into the field.

I wait all night and into the morning. For shouting, pounding feet, accusing fingers. But there is nothing. Do I only dream fire?

I shoulder Bran out of the way, take the bucket. Mara is at the well, her fat babe on one hip. And she has news.

Such a near thing, she says. If not for a wayward gust of wind. If not for a shutter left unlatched. If not for Tunny sitting up late, fretting over his workers' wages. If not, if not.

I fill the bucket and go.

So. Even this is denied me.

I try again. Mara's husband brings down a boar, and she must prepare the meat for smoking, the blood and offal for sausage and pudding. I offer to take care of little Per, and she thanks me, wiping the sweat from her face with a plump forearm.

I take her child into the woods, to the bank of the river. The waters run high, swollen with the heavy rains. I walk out onto the log bridge, holding Per at arm's length. Below, the water boils over smooth-worn stones.

Per waves his arms and dribbles.

I will drop you, I say.

And he chuckles.

Damn. Damn. Damn.

All the way back to the village I coo sweet, soft curse words into the curl of his ear. Perhaps he will out with them later, and his parents will think him a changeling.

I sink into despondency. I am laid in mud like the egg of a wasp. Bran sees how it is with me. Really, we are all ordinary, he says, quiet as though not to rile me.

But they are not. Fartha's hair shines like sunlight on water. It is the colour of honey, always attracting bees. And more than bees. Bran is so clever with animals, they will do anything for him. And Esla sings like a bird, though she has only five years.

I will find her, the one who has done this to me. I will find her, and I will spit her gift back into her face.

My mother tells me since the day she speaks my sentence, she is seen only once, when Tunny's Ama is born. The trestle table groans beneath the weight of the food. The best musicians are hired. Pleased, she gifts the child with a bone from her necklace. The child will ever sew a perfect line, she says.

Not much of a gift, I say. For this I am smacked.

But surely Kelt knows of other appearances. She brings most of the village into this world. Perhaps she catches the Old One wavering over the blood of the child-bed like heated air above a fire. But no. Kelt also does not see her, from that day to this.

Perhaps the Old One is dead, I say.

Hush, or she'll hear you, Kelt says.

So I shout it. The Old One is dead! Sparks fly from the fire, startling us both. But there is nothing more.

Some say the feyen grow fewer, Kelt says, driven out by the subdued earth, the burned fields. Others say they bide their time, get strong in the shadows.

What do you believe, I ask.

She coughs and spits and tells me she is not paid to believe in anything but her two hands and God's fierce mercy. But her mother's mother, she would say that the feyen are with us, around us, even in the light of day, and we do not see them.

How can that be, I ask, and I look quick into the dark corners of her hut, the back of my neck pricking.

She laughs and spits again, and tells me the charm. When a bee flies around you once, twice, thrice, you can see slant, into the cracks between, where the feyen slip in and out. Look around fast, and you might see them, if they are about.

But surely bees fly 'round me, once, twice, thrice, and I see nothing.

Ordinary

Perhaps you don't look right, says Kelt.

You look, and you keep your eyes open, she says. If you blink three times, then it goes.

I leave the eggs, though she gives me nothing of real value.

I am sixteen, and there is to be another child. Fartha is old enough to help. I have become an extra mouth, nothing more. I see it in their eyes when they look at me. I hear them in the night, discussing Reglan, the tanner's son. The thought of it turns my stomach. He is shiftless and lazy. And I cannot abide the stench of their hovel. No one can. That is why they live so far outside the village. Downwind. Downstream.

I have little to gain. But I resolve to try.

At the solstice, musicians come. The brewer pays them a little, but it is not a kindness. For when people dance, they grow thirsty.

Reglan asks me to dance, but I refuse. I feign a hurt ankle, and when he would sit with me I shout at him to go away. It is not his fault, but there is no one else to shout at. I wait, watching the lute player. At last he breaks a string. He places the short end on the bench, and when his back is turned I dart forward to snatch it up. Only Mara sees, but her cheeks are flushed dark with dance and drink, and her gaze slides off me as her partner whirls her away.

From my success I presume that small thieveries are quite commonplace. Ordinary.

Day comes, and I set out — to forage for mushrooms and elderflowers in the woods, I say. But I pursue other prey. I bide my time. I lie down in the warm clover. At last, a bee. And then another. Close to, they are furred, like small, golden bears. I nudge one with my fingertip and am stung for my curiosity. I follow its fellow, squinting into the sun, trying to ignore the pain in my head. And then I see it, their dripping, distended hive clinging to the hollow of an old tree. Always the bees seek the eyes, but none flies around me. Perhaps they know. Perhaps the feyen school them.

The clover wilts between my fingers.

I go home, empty-handed, and I am beaten and sent to bed with no supper. That night my father goes to speak to Reglan's father.

Esla sleeps soundly, and I whisper into Fartha's ear. She ignores me at first, but cannot resist the promise of sweet honey, the colour of her hair. It is easy to find the tree again. I have only to read my own tracks.

Fartha pouts. The nest is too high, she says.

Just wait, I say.

Sure enough, at first light, the bees come, drawn to her hair. I pull her to me, and she struggles in my embrace.

Just wait, I say.

You are ugly, she breathes into my ear. Rage blooms. My hand itches for a knife.

Just then a bee flies around us. I catch my breath. It flies around us again, and then a third time. I hold my eyes open. I look, hard, willing myself to see.

What are you doing, asks Fartha.

Nothing. Go away, I say, releasing her.

But, you promised!

Go away, I say.

She slaps me, hard, and I blink. She stands, breathing heavily. I ignore her. You are ordinary, she shouts. There is not one thing about you that is special.

I know, I say through clenched teeth. But I do not look at her. I want to see.

She leaves. I hear her crashing through the undergrowth like a bull elk.

My eyes water and my cheek burns. I hold my lids up with my fingers. My vision smears. I blink a second time, and curse. Then something comes. It darts and hovers like a hummingbird or a dragonfly, but it is neither of those things. Straight past the bees it flits, into the hive. Then it drops down to a low branch to eat its fill of the broken bit of honeycomb it has stolen. I look away, but step closer. Don't blink. Don't breathe.

Blind cow, I hear something say in a high, tinny voice very near my ear.

Quick as thought, I turn and snatch it from its perch, binding it with the metal string. It shrieks, shrill with rage or fear. I blink, and it is gone, but still I feel it. It is sticky with honey.

Call the Old One, I say. Only she can save your life.

There is more shrieking.

I squeeze my fingers more tightly together. It writhes and squirms. I will kill it, I say.

Suddenly it stills, and I can feel the thudding of its heart beneath my thumb. I realize it is alive. A living creature. Surely, I already know this. But it breaks open in me, the knowing, like something new.

I open my hand, unwind the wire. For a moment there is nothing. Then I feel the whir of wings against my palm, and it is gone. Or so I think. A sharp pain flares on the fleshy pad of my thumb. I swat blindly, but strike nothing. I try to follow, but it moves too quickly, and almost immediately the thin sound is lost to me.

My thumb is throbbing. I make my way to the river, and plunge my hand into its cool waters. The blood that oozes from the wound is the wrong colour. I suck and spit, suck and spit. Blackness falls on me like a smothering blanket. When I wake, the shadows are long and the wound has closed.

Reglan's hands are damp with sweat. His breath smells of beer and onions. He makes his vows to me but looks over my shoulder to where Fartha stands holding a posy of late wildflowers. The women prepare to take me to the tanner's house.

I stop, obstinate. Only Fartha, I say.

They simper. They think I am shy, that I want my sister's comfort. Sparks fly up from the harvest fire. They ring me round, sing a bawdy song with their heads thrown back. I look past the circle, to where my mother stands. Her face is lined and tired and she nurses my newborn brother. They pelt me with millet and barley and Fartha takes my hand. I pull her into the woods.

I need something, I tell her.

Do not worry so, she says. It can be quite pleasant, I hear. She smiles, and it is a sly smile.

Have you seen my husband, I ask.

She shrugs. With their pants down, they all look the same.

I stop and stare at her. She laughs, and looks away.

We come to a clearing, and I know it is near. A little farther on and there is the tree. The bees are silent, sleeping. Do they dream, I wonder. I dig down through layers of sweet, rotting leaves and into the dirt with my broken fingernails. The soil still holds the sun's warmth. From the buried oilskin I pull out a blade, wipe it clean on my skirt. I hold it up so it catches the moonlight.

Whatever do you intend to do with that?

First, I will cut off your hair, I say.

She looks at my face, and her smile slips. Don't be silly.

I grab for her braids, but she yanks her head away and stumbles backwards.

Stop it, she says.

I say nothing, but lunge at her, and she runs, screaming.

I tuck my skirts up under my belt, take up the oilskin, and run in the opposite direction, as fast as I can. At last I come to the river. The rains are late this year, so the water is not too deep. I wade in, try to run, and lose a shoe.

Damn. Damn. Damn.

It is gone in the tumbling water. I hurry, keeping close to the bank, bent double. Beneath the log bridge I stop to catch my breath. The water here rises above my knees, but around the next bend the streambed flattens out again. I limp up onto the dry stones, taking great care not to cut my foot. Blood is too easy to track. Beneath the trees the darkness is nearly complete. Branches scratch my face and hands, catch at my hair. I step on something sharp. A rock, or a broken branch. I go down, cursing. The pain is bad, but I will not cry.

The clouds thin for a moment, and a finger of cold light finds a bee on a mossy log, a hand's breadth from my face.

You should not be out so late, I say. It is too cold, and your hive is far from here. I take it up, breathe warmth onto it. I hear men and dogs. I force myself to my feet and try to walk, but the pain is too much. I fall, bruising my shin on the log. Then it comes to me. I rise again, carefully, the bee cupped in my palm. Hopping on one foot, I turn three times.

Please, I say.

The barking of the dogs rises in pitch.

Please, I say again, holding my eyes open wide. The bee crawls onto my thumb and stings me. I blink and toss it aside.

Old One! I call out. It is too much. Take back your gift. Am I to suffer all my days for my mother's ignorance? For my father's oversight?

There is no reply but for the baying of the dogs. I hear them crashing through the undergrowth. My foot is throbbing now, and my hand is sticky with blood. I blink a second time and suddenly a man appears before me. He is of normal size and stature, but all aglow with a warm, yellow light. Is it an angel, I wonder. He smiles, and I blink, and he disappears.

There! someone shouts. There she is!

Please, I whisper.

Hands take my hands. They are warm and strong and I can smell strawberries, though it is the wrong time of year. The hands pull and I stumble forward, and just as the dogs come upon me I am no longer there. I hear a yelp, but it is far away. And now he stands there, the man, and all around us the sun is shining and the air is full of bees — bees and other flying things — and he is holding my hands.

All right now, he asks.

I open my mouth to answer, but no sound comes. I cannot make sense of it. There before me is the moss-covered log. Behind me is the path I followed, wending its way between thick stands of fir and oak and maple. But the leaves are green and gleaming, not brown and curled. The salmon berry bushes are thick with both fruit and blossoms.

It is the same, but not the same. And where are the men and the dogs? The man drops my hands and I realize neither my foot nor my thumb pain me.

Where am I, I ask. I blink several times, but he is still there.

You are but a half step removed, he says, smiling.

He turns and walks away.

I do not know what else to do, so I pull off my remaining shoe, caked with dirt, and follow.

We come to a clearing. There are more of them gathered here. Some sleep curled together like a litter of kittens. Others play a sort of chase game in the air. Still others recline on heaped-up beds of silks and flowers, feeding one another plump red berries with their fingers.

The sun is pleasantly warm, and I am thirsty. As though hearing my thoughts, the man takes up a shining cup and offers it to me with a bow. Does he mock me?

You may call me Oriel, he says.

If I eat of your food or drink of your wine, I never leave this place, I say.

But why would you not wish to stay, he asks.

I am thrown into confusion again. It has to do with choices, I say. I have had enough of those stolen from me already.

Here there are many choices, he says. Come, drink.

Why do you press me?

He smiles and places the cup in my hand. Because it would please me if you stay, he says.

But why? I am common. And surely this is no place for the ordinary.

He laughs, and I start at the sound. You are not ordinary, he says.

How can you say that? I look around again. In this place, my lack of beauty, of elegance, of charm, seems particularly offensive.

But there is something at which you excel, he murmurs. The others rise from their beds and come around, sniffing at me.

They can smell it on you, he says, how much you want. The yearning comes off you like heat.

They put their faces to my hand and push against my legs like cats. Here we lack nothing. And lacking nothing, we forget how it is to want. Come, he says, remind us.

I need to think, I say.

He puts his lips to my ear. But I hear you. You beg to leave that place. You call upon the Old One.

Where is she? Take me to her!

Your kind is always in a hurry, he says, yawning.

If she will not show herself, then I will not stay.

You are quite sure? He makes an odd gesture with his hand and something black opens up before me. I hear the shouting of men, the barking of dogs. I step back quickly. Do not fear, he says, they cannot see you.

But how can that be, for I can see and hear them as clear as day, though with them it is still night. The dogs mill about excitedly while the men beat the bushes, calling out. And here is Reglan. He takes up my oilskin. A stale loaf of bread falls out, and a length of Mara's blood pudding. He looks up, and seems to look directly at me.

She does not mean to be my wife at all, he says, and his lips thin into an angry line. He picks up my knife, weighing it in his hand, then he drives it into the trunk of a nearby tree.

The Old One, I whisper, still watching Reglan, she is truly here?

Where else would she be, Oriel says, not answering me.

But it does not matter. I look at the tanner's son and raise the cup to my lips, and I drink long and deep.

The feyen move neither forward nor back. Everything that has been or will be flows around them, and they remain, unchanged and unchanging, like flies in amber.

But a half step removed, time travels differently. I watch the others through the hole in the air. Fartha's hair is darker, and her middle thicker. She births two healthy boys, and grows restless. Bran lives alone with his dogs, and follows Tunny's Ama with his eyes. I know he thinks he is not good enough for her. But really, he is too good. Mother is gone, and Esla does not sing so often.

I eat less and sleep more.

When Fartha's grandchild has four or five winters, Oriel takes my hand and leads me along a path I have not seen before. We come to a small cottage with a garden. The feyen neither build nor plant, so I am curious. An old woman works the soil. It is strange to see something so tattered and stooped here. When she sees us she straightens her back with an effort. Oriel takes her hand, her filthy split-nailed hand, and bends over it like a courtier. She pulls the scarf from her head to wipe her brow, and I see the shorn grey hair, the heavy-lidded eyes.

It is the Old One, I whisper, disbelieving.

Come, she says. There is tea. It helps with the lethargy.

Oriel is not there when I turn. It vexes me, this way he has of being there and then not there. The old anger wakes in my gut. Do you wish to poison me as well, I say to her. To finish the work?

What work is that, she asks.

You know full well. The work of destroying my life!

She turns and goes into her cottage. I follow, trembling with rage. She laughs, and I see she has no teeth. She hands me a chipped cup full of hot, fragrant tea. I quell the urge to throw it at her. Look where you are, girl, she says. Is your beautiful sister here? Or Tunny's coddled Ama? Is it some clever teacher who spins tales for the feyen?

I sit, suddenly tired again. That is not the point, I say.

Then what is?

You have stolen my choices from me, made me what I am not.

Child. How do you know what you are, what you could be? I only stir up what is already there. I only breathe on that fire in your belly, give you an enemy, so you try harder. See?

I think on this for a moment. But what if I fail, I ask. One blink, and I am with Reglan now, bearing his brats in the stink of his hovel.

Who do you think sends the bee, she asks. And Oriel, to bring you through?

I am quiet. That breathless flight through the woods, it is another life, now.

She shakes her head. You will not fail. I hear it in your bawling the moment you enter the world. You see enough birthings, you know the ones. They announce their arrival. They fight, and want, and seek. And she who seeks, if she seeks with all her heart, finds. See?

No, I say. It may be that I begin to. Only I am still angry. So I put down the tea, untasted, and go away.

In the shade of a rowan I watch as Bran breathes his last. Esla weeps over his body, wiping her tears from his face with her long, grey hair. My face, also, is wet. I sleep, and wake, and watch as a butterfly creeps from its cocoon, its wings trembling and useless. Soon it flits about the hollyhocks, though there is no one to show it how.

I find Oriel. Show me again the way to the Old One, I say.

She is gone, he says with a shrug.

Gone? Gone where?

Only gone. In the way of your kind. It is slower here, but still it comes.

I do not believe you, I say through clenched teeth, though I have never known him to lie to me outright.

He shows me her cottage. Already it is falling into disrepair. I want to weep, though with rage or grief, I cannot say.

But I want—I begin, and then I stop. I do not know what I want now.

Oriel takes up something from the table and places it in my hands: a half-dozen glittering, uncut gems fixed to a circlet of dull silver. It is yours now, he says. The stones are cold against my skin. I turn to go, and find that the others are there with us, crowding 'round. Come, Oriel says, tell us a story.

On the day that Per's newborn two-greats-granddaughter is to be named, I am ready. I have taken to wearing my hair shorn close, and my cloak of raven's feathers is finished. My nails are broken and stained with the black soil of my garden, where I grow the herbs for the Old One's tea.

I am not invited, for they have let the old ways slip again. It does not matter, and it is not why I go, but I know it is to be a part of the story.

I make the sign in the air and step through. There is fear on the faces surrounding me. The parents beg and plead, but their voices are like the whine of insects in my ears.

I stretch out my hand.

The child, I say, will be wholly ordinary.

And they do not know. Is this a curse? Or a blessing?

For my part, I know. I know exactly.

HE HAD THIS THING

James Norcliffe

New Zealand poet **James Norcliffe** has published nine collections of poetry including Shadow Play (2013) and Dark Days at the Oxygen Café (2016). Recent work has appeared in Landfall, Spillway, The Cincinnati Review, Salamander, Gargoyle and Flash Fiction International (Norton, 2015). In 2010 he took part in the XX International Poetry Festival in Medellin, Colombia, and in 2011 the Trois Rivières International Poetry Festival in Québec.

*H*E HAD THIS THING

He had this thing about flies.
It started with the compound eyes so perfectly compartmentalized. He saw them as textured goggles with thousands of three-dimensional pixels. Hell's angels. Goggles and eyes upon eyes. He obsessed how they could capture him in reverse micro images which they would reassemble to form fly-pictures, flies-eye views of him. Even as they were flying.
She tried to ignore it.
Even as they were whining and zigzagging erratically across the room.
When he swung at them they accelerated and the whine became angry.
Their anger angered him.
She told him to ignore them.
They were wearing goggle-like fly masks hiding their fly identities.
She told him to stop it.
And when they were still, nothing improved.
Their standing on vertical surfaces was improbably perverse, but real.

Their ability to walk upside down on the ceiling even more so.
She told him to shut the screen door.

And he hated their thoraxes almost as much as he hated the word thorax. When he said the word, it sounded like dried coffee grounds in his mouth. Thorax. Thorax.

And their brown, brittle exoskeletons. Unsoft. Unfleshly. Unwarm.

Go for a walk, she said. They're getting to you.

They vomit, he said. Digest, then vomit and digest again.

Think of something else, she said.

He tried.

Eggs.

More eggs.

Maggots.

GUARDIAN

Susan Pieters

Susan Pieters *has an MA in English from the days when she had more time (that is, before she had kids.) She now lives in BC with her supportive spouse (who knew writing was so expensive?) and her always-not-quite-adult children (how hard can it be to help with the dishes?). She spends her time writing fiction and editing for* Pulp Literature. *She is the winner of the* 2017 *Cedric Award for memoir, and her fiction can be found in* Tesseracts 20, Compostela *(Edge,* 2017*) and* Analog *(forthcoming). To attend her workshops or meet her in person at writing conferences, sign up for the newsletter at pulpliterature.com.*

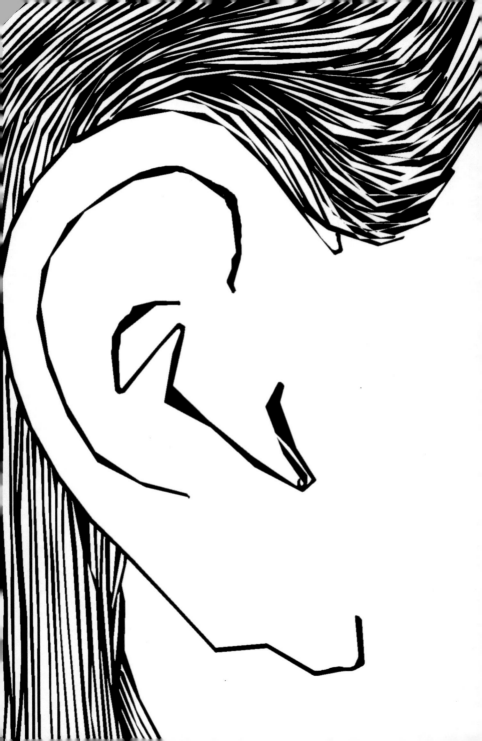

GUARDIAN

I tapped at my Guardian earpiece and lifted my eyebrows.

The man standing behind the counter gave me a once-over before he checked the front door cam. We were alone. "You want it unlocked?"

I nodded. The sign outside the shop said 'Cell Phones Unlocked'. But word on the street — or under the street — was that they could do much more than cell phones.

"Why?" He crossed his arms. They were tattooed like in a retro movie, from the days when people rebelled against conformity by self-mutilation. Those days were gone now, thanks to the device in my ear.

When I didn't answer, he asked me again. "Why do you want it unlocked? You want to jump off the Second Narrows Bridge?"

I debated how to answer. Claiming I was suicidal might be the easiest ticket to an unlocked Guardian. There was a strong element of society that maintained the individual's right to end their own life, despite the secondary mandate against self-harm.

It was the primary mandate that people were more concerned with.

"No jumping. But don't worry. I don't plan to blow away some school kids, if that's what you're asking."

The tatted arms crossed. "That is exactly what I'm asking. I need reasons. Good ones."

"You won't believe me." I tried to stare him down.

His eyes flickered a honey brown. I wondered how old he was. Was his Guardian setting on high or low?

What would it be like to have the electrical implant turned down, to have no security fence around one's life? No one had been able to tell me. All citizens had them — and non-citizens were kept out by a much larger electrical fence. It was what kept our country safe.

"If you're a student trying to protest free will, you're welcome to renounce your citizenship. Go to the Outside. Be wild and free forever. I just hope you're good with a shovel, because I hear they eat a lot of vegetables there."

"It's not for political reasons. It's personal. It's . . . not for the reasons you think."

"How do you know what I think?" He turned his back to me, pulling out a log book. "I've heard them all, sister. How about this one?" He flipped the book open to a random page in the middle and read aloud. "'I'm tired of feeling safe all the time. I need some risk.' That one I adjusted slightly so she could perform better in races. She pushed herself — and her car — into an early grave. Didn't take much. At least it was only a secondary mandate violation. Didn't harm anyone but herself."

I looked down at the display of prepaid phone cards. The fact he'd told me this meant he wasn't afraid of me. He didn't even think I would tell the cops. I was like a bot to him. "Okay. I'll show you."

Stepping around the counter, I took the book out of his hand and dropped it on the counter. The pages fell open. I looked at them briefly before closing the cover; the handwritten scrawl was hard to read but for the word 'Guardian' that repeated like an illness, or a diagnosis, on the page.

He crossed his arms again. He was taller up close. "You going to try and steal something?"

My answer was to put my finger on his forearm and trace the blue and teal feathers of his phoenix. I ran my fingertip over the vermilion flames that wrapped up towards his elbow. The copper-coloured hair on his arms made the image three-dimensional. He had found a good tattoo artist.

I had the man's attention, but I didn't look into his eyes. Not yet.

I went higher and caressed his shoulder. He had muscles under his T-shirt.

"What are you playing at, girl?"

"Hush. It's a demonstration."

"Of what?" He fell silent as my hands wrapped around his neck.

He wasn't afraid. How could he be, when he knew my Guardian settings were at full power? I could no more hurt him than I could fly into space. But still, he shivered.

My fingers dragged over the rough stubble on his chin and cheeks, which was also reddish, despite the dark curls at the nape of his neck. My fingers explored his earlobe and the gold earring he had somehow managed to insert below his own Guardian earpiece. I looked into his eyes.

He wasn't as old as I'd thought at first. His shop was dark, which was important for business, but his eyes were bright with wariness and questions.

I leaned closer. "May I?" It was a forced question, thanks to my new generation Guardian.

He didn't say anything, just held his breath as I put my lips on his. They were just lips. The touch of his face against mine was nothing special, like a hot water bottle pressed against me, like a comforting placebo of sterile human interaction.

I pulled back slightly. "What do you feel?"

His eyes were working, shifting like I had turned a kaleidoscope and shaken up the colours. "I feel —" He stopped himself. "What do you feel?"

"I feel safe." I was too angry to cry. "I always feel safe. Like I'm going to bed with milk and cookies, not with somebody that I love, not with —"

"You want it dangerous?" He tugged his T-shirt out of my grasp. "Don't use birth control."

I wanted to slap him, but I couldn't. "I want it real," I said.

"Why would 'real' be dangerous?"

"Because it's a risk." I saw something flicker again in his eyes. "Yours is adjusted down, isn't it?" Then the shoe dropped. "Is yours turned off?"

He didn't deny it. "I couldn't do this work otherwise."

"I want what you feel."

"Sure you do." He said it like he disagreed, but he glanced over to check his front door cam, and then he bent over me and his kiss was what I'd read about in books: hungry, like a wolf. Dangerous and unpredictable. If his Guardian was turned off, this man could do anything to me he pleased—not that he would. He didn't automatically turn into a rapist serial killer once he'd been left to his own human nature—but he could do other things, selfish things, hurtful things. He could love me and leave me with a broken heart.

He pulled back. "Satisfied?"

I shook my head. "More."

His tongue was inside my mouth like he was exploring for who I was, and I wanted him to find me. I wanted to give in and give up and give him who I truly was—

That's when my Guardian kicked in, protecting me. Keeping my identity and my personhood safe. Intact.

He felt it. He pulled back. "What the hell?" He sounded confused.

I had tears in my eyes. I had come so close to real desire, to real love. Crazy to think, in five minutes, that somebody could fall in love. Crazy, like this whole idea.

His hand was cradling the device on my ear. "When did you get this? Recently?"

"Last month. It's the newest model."

"Is this the androgynous version, or did they . . ." He pulled a tool out of his pocket. Before I knew it, cold air rushed into my left ear canal, which had been covered over since I could remember. The street noise on that side felt oddly loud yet far away.

"You took it out?" I said stupidly.

He had it under a microscope already, opened up. "I used to work for Bell Bio. If they've . . ." He looked back over at me. "Before I do this, let's test the theory. It could be something else, you know. Not your Guardian."

He didn't explain what else it might be. He just wiped his hands on his jeans. Was he sweating?

My own hands were cool, and my ear felt naked.

"Try again?" he asked, coming near.

I blinked the wetness from my eyes. "Yes, I want this." I spoke out of habit, even though the Guardian was out.

The kiss started slow, almost cold. His lips were tight and tense. Mine felt numb. Then there was warmth, like sunshine hitting a lake, when you can suddenly see the depths and swimming fish and then you hear birdsong.

His lips were like the eagle coming down out of the sky, like an eagle that can see a beetle sharply from a mile in the air, and he dives towards you—

We had our clothes off before he remembered to bolt the front door.

"I found you," he whispered and kissed my left ear, the naked one.

I pressed myself to him in the dark.

He'd unlocked everything.

FIVE MINUTES

Jasmin Nyack

Jasmin Nyack *refuses to confirm whether or not she has ever been captured by aliens. But something must be the cause of her newfound hobbies of sword fighting, baking, and knitting Weasley-inspired sweaters. She will confirm that this story is inspired by the endless love she has for the many moms in her life who make it look so easy. Jasmin currently resides in Vancouver, BC, where she is finishing her Creative Writing degree.*

$\mathcal{F}$IVE MINUTES

"Can we listen to music?" Ethan whined from the back seat, curling up in a blanket.

"Of course we can, sweetheart. Max, could you put the iPod in?" Tracey asked her husband, her voice a forced calm as the driver in front of them began to have a melt down. The driver started crying and pulling out her hair. Tracey could hear the small sound of shrieking over the engines and cars and into her own car. As Max turned on the music and fell back against his seat, Disney tunes drowned out the noises outside.

Tracey watched the woman, turned on the car blinkers, and waited to merge into the next lane. And waited. And waited. The crescendo of the cinematic music was flattened by an additional nasal horn-blast. Tracey looked at Max and the piles of used tissues in front of his seat as he dropped another one.

"Could you not?" Tracey snapped. "Put your garbage into a bag."

"What bag?" Max moaned.

Tracey tightened her jaw, keeping her eye on the road, and began to look for an empty bag in the mess of the car. As the woman in the silver Kia, the type Tracey usually saw in grocery stores with perfect makeup, began to howl, Tracey wondered if the woman, too, had a husband and two children with the flu as aliens decided to invade. That or there was a certain privilege of insanity that came without the extra tissues and sniffles echoing in the car. When she grabbed something wet, Tracey wrinkled her nose, pushed it aside, and kept searching as the traffic sat still on the busy highway. She found a plastic bag with nothing in it and waved it at Max. Tracey blew her own nose as more cars crawled forward and horns wailed behind them. Tracey leaned her forehead against the leather steering wheel and held in a moan of misery as her sinuses started to pound below and above her eyes. Was it too much to ask for five minutes of peace and quiet?

"Mom!" Mattie called from the back, "Let me out!"

"Sorry, sweetie, we have to wait just a bit longer," Tracey said, looking at the toddler whose screwed-up face was turning red. Tracey prayed to whatever deity may have been listening that Mattie could keep it together. "Let's listen to Moana!"

"I don't wanna listen to Moana. I don't like Moana," Ethan complained, her son's voice a long, drawn-out whine.

"Moana!" Mattie called, clapping her hands together.

"No!"

"Moana!"

"*No!*" Ethan shouted back.

"Ethan, calm down. We'll listen to one song," Tracey said, pulling the car around the vehicle in front that no longer seemed able to move forward. "And then we can listen to something you want." She tapped her fingers, wishing she could turn on the public radio to learn what was going on. Was the world crumbling around them? Was it a false alarm? Looking at the clear, blue sky around them, it was unthinkable that the warning was real. But Tracey craned her neck around the car, past her blind spots, trying to see to see something.

"Why does Mattie always get everything?" Ethan cried.

"You like Moana."

"No, I don't."

"Let's listen to Maui," Tracey said, her forced calm crackling around the edges. "Max, could you put on Maui?"

A superhero instrumental floated through the car, the crescendo rising and falling. Nothing changed, not even the clicking noise of someone looking through the long playlist. Tracey turned her eyes from the road to Max. He was fast asleep, his cheek pressed against the window, mouth open, oblivious to it all.

She let out a breath, took her eyes off the road for a moment, and tried to find the song. But before she found it, Mattie began to have a fit in her car seat. Ethan whined. As the song cried, *You're Welcome*, both kids cried louder. Tracey ground her teeth and felt the pressure all the way to the top of her head as it pushed up on her sinuses.

Both the kids screamed at each other.

"Will you two shut up!" Max jolted awake, turning around his seat to face the kids.

And now both kids were howling. Tracey threw a look at Max.

"What?" Max said. "They are out of control."

"And they're sick, stuck in a car, and unhappy. Of course they are out of control. You are too."

"I am not out of control," he snarled.

"Yes, you are." Tracey said, grabbing another tissue to blow her nose.

"Well, it's not like I planned this."

"I never said you did. I want to be in bed too and not stuck in this damn gridlock."

A shadow fell over them and the cars in front of them. Silence fell in the car and snuffed out the screams and protests as everyone looked up at the giant black ship that flew over them. Blue lights shone out to the side, bright and painful to look at, but their cold glow did not touch the highway. As one glided past like a slick oil spill another took its place, hovering over them. The huge black ships landed with a silent motion beside the highway, but the field grasses all bowed away from the monstrous winds.

Emergency vehicles of all sorts blared their sirens, snapping the silence in two, and then billions, of pieces. Police cars with whirling blue and red lights drove along the side of the road, forcing themselves between the civilians and the aliens. Dozens more, ambulances and search and rescue trucks, pulled up on the other side of the highway in the open meadow.

"Police cars!" Ethan proclaimed, pressing his snotty face to the window.

"Yeah, buddy . . . police cars." Max drifted off, his skin ashen as well as green.

People got out of their cars. Some looked up and pointed, some merely watched. Others shrieked in hysterics, running away from the ships and their own cars as fast as they could. Some sobbed inside of their cars, holding on to those with them. A few teenagers took pictures with their cell phones.

The ships glowed for a moment, their lights blue, then a large ramp lowered to the ground. Mattie began banging her feet on her car seat, screaming the whole while. Ethan was entranced by the emergency vehicles. The spaceships' thrumming was low and created a new pressure inside her head alongside the one from her sinuses as the last dregs of Nyquil worked their way out of her system. Tracey knew that she should be more concerned with the fact that aliens had come to take over the planet, but she couldn't think through the growing mess in her head. She just wanted her own bed and a moment of quiet. These aliens just felt like an inconvenience. Tracey put her fingers to the bridge of her nose and took a few deep breaths.

Aliens. Tall—no, huge creatures with black shiny exoskeleton skin crawled out of the spaceships in twos. Their four legs clicked with Nazi precision as they walked down their gangplanks and lined up. They had strange crab-like claws sheathed in glowing, metal weapons that they fired at the police who stood too close. The officers turned into dust, and Ethan was suddenly much quieter as the aliens turned towards the largest ship. The largest of the crab-like aliens stepped out, with carvings all along the shell of its body, eye stalks swirling, mandibles grinding along each other, teeth visible beyond them.

The sirens, the sounds of the aliens, and the yelling of the police and terrified people mixed in with Ethan and Mattie's wailing over the music and rattled into Tracey's head. Max was speaking with barely contained terror, but his voice was just one more sound in the cacophony, and Tracey barely heard a word he said. The din clanged in her head, building the pressure behind her eyes. Max hollered at the kids to quiet down as their sick cries grew into panicked ones. Ethan and Mattie responded by shrieking ever louder. The sounds of Max blowing his nose were mixed with Ethan coughing deeply. And then a police officer started talking to the crowd through a large megaphone that squealed randomly.

"Enough!" Tracey slammed her hands down on the steering

wheel and threw open the car door. Max and the children fell silent in an instant. Tracey untangled herself from the seatbelt and stepped onto the highway. "Stay in the car."

The road, however, was still filled with noise that hit her like a brick. Screaming, swearing, and sobbing echoed with the thrumming of the ships and the sounds of car engines. As Tracey marched across the road, she ripped a tire iron out of a man's hand. She marched towards the black orbs and their crab-like aliens.

"Ma'am!" a police officer said, holding a shaking hand out to stop her. "Ma'am, you must go back. We ... we have this covered." He swallowed as Tracey kept marching forward. He grabbed her arm, "Ma'am—"

"Get out of my way, Officer." Tracey's voice was level and cool as she ripped her arm out of his grasp. She kept marching forward. The officer watched wordlessly as she went.

Tracey marched across the field and didn't flinch as the weapons of the crab creatures turned in her direction. Her pace was steady, and she only stopped once she stood in front of the black crab with the carving on his shell. With a single move, she threw the tire iron into the monster and the shell cracked. The crab stopped its clicking speech and swivelled two eye stalks in her direction. The other aliens shuffled back. The tire iron fell with a clatter in front of Tracey, and the area finally fell silent.

Tracey picked up the tire iron and waved it in the direction of the alien commander. "You will get back on that ship and leave and never come back." The crab began to click again but Tracey waved the iron. "You will listen to me when I am talking!" The crab took a step back and stopped his clicking. "You have five minutes to get back on that ship, or so help me god!"

In a moment of rage, she swung her iron at the creature's front leg, taking it down.

Then Tracey turned away and started marching back to her van, with every person on the highway watching her. She stopped and turned back. "If you do come back, I will destroy you and have you for my dinner!"

She turned and marched back to her car. Past the startled officer who had stopped her, his eyes bugging out of his head. Past the man whose tire iron she had stolen. She dropped it at his feet with a short, "Thank you," and got back in the van.

No one made a sound. Neither Mattie nor Ethan seemed to have a sound in them, and Max stared at her in open-mouthed horror as Tracey buckled herself in and put her mom smile back on. "Let's go home," she announced, then started the van, signalled, and than backed up. She pulled a U-turn and drove down the open grass and away from the aliens. She didn't look back. When the roads cleared, she merged back onto the road and followed the stoplights back to their suburban home.

Tracey pulled into the local supermarket. "Just sit tight for five minutes. I'm going to grab some things."

Leaving her stunned family in the car, Tracey walked into the empty supermarket. No one was there, but it was a disaster. Broken pasta jars and empty cardboard lay everywhere, but the store still had stock. She picked up two bottles of cold medicine and multiple boxes of tissues. One of the boxes she opened right away and lustily blew her nose on the aloe-softened tissue. She grabbed juice and soft foods. Tracey did the math in her head and left a note and precise change on the register. She bagged the groceries and took an extra cloth bag to help.

Tracey put the groceries in the car. "One more, and then we can go home." She turned and walked into the liquor store. She tiptoed as best she could over the destroyed bottles and grabbed a Johnny Walker black label. Rummaging in her purse, she didn't find enough, so left what she could and another note.

Their house, with fading blue siding and toy-strewn yard, came into view, and Tracey let out a breath of relief. Pulling into the driveway, with its grungy garage door, she had never been so happy to see so much to do.

"We're home!" she called. With Max still looking at her in disbelief, Tracey got out of the car and unbuckled the sleeping toddler, hooking with one finger the bag of groceries that contained the whiskey. Mattie snuffled and snorted in her sleep as the door clicked open, and the scent of home washed over them: the cheesy, diaper smell of a living family. Laying Mattie on the couch, she stepped back into the kitchen, poured herself a drink of whiskey, and leaned against the dish-covered counters.

"Mom!" Ethan screamed. "Mattie threw up on the couch!"

THE POTATO BUG WAR

Charity Tahmaseb

Charity Tahmaseb *has slung corn on the cob for Green Giant and jumped out of airplanes (but not at the same time). She's worn both Girl Scout and Army green. These days, she writes fiction and works as a technical writer in St. Paul, Minnesota. Her short fiction credits include stories in* Deep Magic, Escape Pod, Cicada, *and* Pulp Literature. *She's been nominated twice for a Pushcart Prize Award, and her first novel (* The Geek Girl's Guide to Cheerleading*) was a YALSA 2012 Popular Paperback pick in the Get Your Geek On category. She blogs occasionally at writingwrongs.blog.*

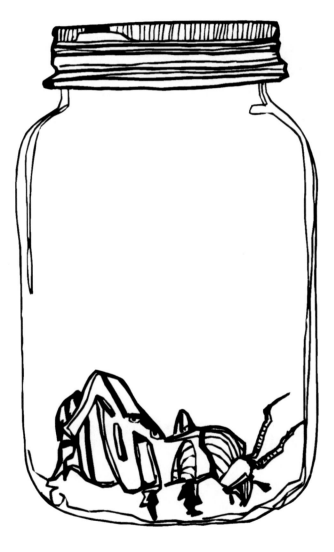

The Potato Bug War

Her students collected so many potato bugs that Emilienne had to dash back to the vineyard for an extra wagon and a pram, all under the glare of a German soldier. The pram squeaked its protest, the wheels jolting along ruts while Henri's words rang in her head:

Make it a game. Let the children have some fun.

So Emilienne handed each of her charges a jar and sent them into the potato fields under the hot Burgundy sun.

"Whoever collects the most wins a sweet!"

The children scampered through the fields, hands greedy for the tiny bugs. The damage was minimal—for now. But a blight was a blight, the potato crop at risk. As Henri put it:

Can't deprive les Boches *of their pommes frites, can we now?*

Her students bent and plucked. One girl stumbled across the furrows, jar clutched to her chest in triumph.

"Mademoiselle! Look how many I've collected!"

The girl ran off with another jar but turned before resuming her spot in the field. "Will it be enough?"

Emilienne patted her skirt pocket, the one with the sweet. "We'll see."

She arranged the jars in the wagons, glass scraping against metal, sun baking the striped creatures inside. They crawled over each other, all in search of an opening that was no longer there.

So many bugs, and yet, she wondered, how many did the Germans expect them to collect? Would it be enough? How much *was* enough when it came to potato bugs?

In the end, she awarded the sweet to the industrious little girl. The child's two older brothers lugged the wagons into town while Emilienne pushed the pram. The jars rocked and clattered, her strange, many-legged babies squirming. Sweat trickled down her spine, and a taste, like rusty grit, filled her mouth.

At the turn-in point, a lone soldier waited. He was no more than a boy, this German, this Nazi. In her head, she heard Henri: *Poor bastard probably has to count them all.*

"What will you do with them?" Emilienne knew better than to start a conversation. She wasn't a collaborator. And no matter how much her belly rumbled at night, she wouldn't accept those kinds of favours.

Still, she wanted to know. As if the fate of these potato bugs mattered to her, to Burgundy, to the war.

"Drown them." The boy grimaced as if he, personally, was responsible for the task.

Poor bastard, indeed.

In the end, she relinquished all but one jar. It was such a foolish thing to do, hiding it there beneath the pram's tattered cushion. Would they line up a firing squad? Shoot her? Perhaps, but only after the Gestapo had their turn.

Tell me, Fraulein, why have you deprived the Reich of these potato bugs?

Yes, why had she? Emilienne couldn't say. That didn't stop her from gathering potato leaves from the field. That night, in the

wine cellar, she stabbed the lid with an ice pick. She shoved hand-
fuls of leaves into the jar and fed her hungry, many-legged babies.

That summer, whenever she overheard the Germans complain
about the harvest, Emilienne thought of a jar, hidden in the wine
cellar, and swallowed a smile.

It was enough.

TOWING THE MUSTANG

Keltie Zubko

Every year we publish the winner and runners-up of the Surrey International Writers' Conference Storyteller's Award. This story was one of the two runners-up as chosen by Jack Whyte and Diana Gabaldon at SiWC 2017.

Keltie Zubko is a Western Canadian writer who divides her time between Vancouver Island and Alberta. She has an extensive background writing about freedom of speech legal cases, but now prefers to explore our human relationship with technology in her short stories and novels.

SIWC Storyteller's Award
Honourable Mention:
Towing the Mustang

Taking her for a spin on the highway, testing her ability to fit comfortably into the bland and rushing traffic might be pushing his luck. At least he could head out to the beach nearby and park close enough to see the ocean without dragging his unreliable leg over the sandy, bumpy ground. The car might get people to stop and talk for awhile, but if there were no tourists, at least he could watch the sailboats skim past on the bright straits to the harbour, while he sipped a coffee, reclined deep in the seat that embraced him with comfortable memories.

The restored Mustang coughed a bit as he pulled her up to the gas pumps, nice and easy, top down, red paint glistening in the summer sun. She'd jerked and sputtered a couple of times since leaving his son's garage that morning, but maybe all she needed was a run on the highway. First, she had to have gas. He would stay on the roads close to his new neighbourhood, where they'd stuck him in the basement suite that came with half of the garage as a condition he'd move there. The place was cramped and unfamiliar but near the strip mall where his friends in the classic car group gathered on Saturday evenings all summer long.

He let the kid at the gas bar do the work, not having to tell him where to find the tank, for a change. All the restored muscle cars came there for gas on Saturdays, late in the afternoon when the informal "show and shine" took over the parking lot after most businesses closed for the day. The kids that worked there were inured to the parade of heavy, old cars of novel colour and design. Sometimes they were mildly curious, but at least they didn't treat the drivers like freaks amid the energy-efficient SUVs and compacts in their repetitive, understated colours.

He was glad he didn't have to serve himself and test his trick knee. He settled in to the seat reupholstered like the original. The hum of cars coming and going and the occasional drift of music or conversation lay like gentle white noise over him. He waited for the tank to fill, while the kids dashed around serving multiple customers at once. He peered across the line-up to the other side of the pumps and saw her. Of course, he had to look right into the eyes of that aging babe in the rusted-out Barracuda fuelling up, too. He looked away. He didn't even know her name. She wasn't technically part of the club, but she always seemed to show up on Saturdays when the collectible cars met.

The thing was, her car wasn't restored. It was kindly referred to as a 'survivor'. He noticed that as usual, she was alone. On the weekends, she always parked across the lot, halfway stalking the group, sometimes joining them, but usually hanging back among the regular patrons of the strip mall going about their regular business, getting groceries or rushing in to one of the stores about to close for a Saturday night. Meanwhile, the shiny procession of relics arrived one by one, some flashy and roaring, others sedate, rolling in with dignity. They settled into the choicest spots to show off the investment of work, love, and money in metal, paint, and memories. With some guys came their original wives, dressed to go cruising, who remembered when the muscle cars were new, or younger second wives, who didn't.

The one with the Barracuda, in her late sixties, he thought, mingled with them, but shrugged off their advice about repairs and bodywork or a new paint job on the car that a few of them coveted. It wasn't a '71, for sure, but striking enough in its own right, even though not a convertible like his Mustang. Any guy owning that car would never have brought it to the Saturday night gatherings in that shape: rusted and ailing, needing some attention and care instead of still being used as her everyday ride. Sometimes people would peer inside the interior as if it was part of the show, but she'd shoo them away from the torn seats, sun-bleached roof, and missing chrome letters that left a shadow of the real word on its bumper.

He chanced another look at her, but she was talking to the attendant, smiling a generic smile, the kind he'd seen young girls fake at old guys like him. He'd seen that look on her face at the car show, amid the old cars backed into their spaces. Placards rested on the dashboards announcing their provenance, and refurbished insides awaited inspection by the women. Gaping hoods beckoned the men to peer at the engines, sometimes chromed, always flaunting new parts. Meanwhile, the owners absorbed admiration as if they could transfer some of it back into their own bodies.

He looked away from her and remained sitting in his Mustang, where he fit the seat like he'd been formed by it instead of the other way around, like with those modern seats with their strategic padding and support, designed by engineers dedicated to human well-being. True, the seats today were attractive, safe and comfortable, but none of them, not even the highest end sports car, could give him the feeling of getting into his 1968 Mustang.

It wasn't just the seat and the materials. Ducking down to climb inside that particular car, despite his knee that gave out at times, his thickened hands and tricky joints, he felt something come back to him that was otherwise lost and almost forgotten. He fed his body into the machine like his soul donning its exoskeleton, as he put on the armour for his exposed widower's heart, or a coat of steel bravado for the lust of his teenage memories.

He closed his eyes a second while the attendant passed the Mustang, rushing to the cars behind him. They were busy today, just another normal day for everyone else but him.

The air freshener wafted its pine scent back at him. He'd never go for the exotic array of scents available now. The heat of the day wasn't so bad yet, here at the gas bar, but would intensify later, plaster his skin to the seat, especially if he took off down the highway and headed to a beach farther out. There was no air conditioning, but if he made it to the ocean, parked by the water to watch the sailboats and tourists promenade by, a breeze would unstick both his flesh and his memories from the empty passenger seat.

He looked down at his wrinkled hands, thickened slightly at a few joints, resting on the old steering wheel that felt so small compared to newer ones. It felt like a woman's delicate bones: not heavy and cushioned, instead hard and perhaps a bit brittle, but with dips and bumps in the plastic for his fingers to fit right into, maybe at one time, even, to caress. He'd taken the top down for such a sunny day. It might be windy on the highway, and perhaps he could taste a slight salty breeze off the ocean. That same ocean once called them all from their cruising downtown, through the velvet summer nights to the beach, to park and drink and neck. That's what they'd done in those days.

He looked up to catch the sun glancing off the shiny red hood, feeling the structure of the car clasp his body so he didn't have to rely on his own failing bones, especially his knee that gave out with a sudden reminder of time and the cost of everything. His balance came and went these days. He might still know his engines, but he couldn't always do anything about it by himself.

He wanted to swing the car hard to the right and pull out of the line-up away from the incessant hurrying at the mall, where everyone moved so fast, eyes slid over him, over his restored car like she was just another recent model, interchangeable in grey or beige, white or black. He wanted to pull her out and hit the highway, away from the young with their attention always on their phones. It was much different from the Saturday show and shine, the leisurely pace when the stores closed, the cars pulled in, the owners dawdled among the colourful throwbacks, occupying the same space, asserting their rights and their past, their legacy and their heritage, all invisible to those who hadn't yet lived it. You could almost remember what your buddies looked like then, as teenagers. The wives, who'd raised families and were grandmothers now, acted like girls, ready to go for a joyride to the beach instead of heading home too damn early.

There she waited in her decrepit Barracuda, pointed in the opposite direction but right in his line of vision if he turned his head, again, just slightly. Her car always seemed to need oil. Finally the kid came back to him, put the gas cap back so he could leave. He turned the key to get the hell out of there and on his way. But instead of a roar, he heard a feeble click, an impotent 'click, click,' as he turned the key again. No life, not even a cough.

He'd have to get out of the car now, and was glad that the Barracuda was still busy getting oil. He opened the heavy door, waiting for it to swing and not rebound on his leg, then climbed up like pulling his soft inner soul out of its metal casing for the young people at the gas station to gaze upon and judge. He straightened up and felt a bit of pressure on his knees, but he'd remembered to put the brace on before he left, and it held. Still, he moved carefully. Always now, when he first got up, he tottered just a little bit. But he had a bigger problem, stuck in the busy line-up, the Mustang dead.

The kid saw him, hurried back over, and together they lifted the hood. He knew these guys, gas jockeys not mechanics, most of them. They could do nothing but wiggle a few things, test connections, look for leaks. Still she wouldn't start. He sighed, and felt the Barracuda focusing on him from over his right shoulder.

His Mustang, meanwhile, didn't even sigh.

"Can you call me a tow truck?"

"Sure, but first we'll push it out of the way."

A couple of the others materialized to do the job without relying on him amid the waiting cars. He couldn't help them, just had to watch while they manhandled her, careful with her shiny paint, moving her out of the stream of restless customers. The young guys were casual about their strength, like he once had been, not realizing its ephemeral advantage, as if they were thinking, "Muscle cars? So what?" They had their own muscles, and thought they'd last forever.

He gave a sideways glance at the Barracuda, her hood raised with its sun-faded turquoise paint, the original paint that seemed to hold the whole thing together. That figures, he thought. She still hasn't done anything about those leaking seals. Right when he thought about it and glanced over, she looked at him again, and this time he nodded in acknowledgement. She smiled a small smile back at him, her lipstick worn down to muted pink.

As the young guys guided his Mustang into a parking spot where the tow truck could reach it, he heard the Barracuda start up with its usual growl and knew without looking there would be a brief flood of blue-grey smoke. At least it started and ran, pulling away from the line-up where he was stranded.

Maybe she did pollute the air, but he still felt the power of that engine reverberating in his bones and wondered if she did, too. Those engines roared and purred about a past age that would never come again. They were icons now, overrun by those that made almost no sound at all but crept around as if fearful to announce their presence. Not hers, that's for sure. He had to admire its sound, starting like that, saying, "Here I am, take me as I am, I don't care what you think, you don't know it all."

The young guys returned to their customers. One went into the office and called the tow truck. Waiting on the sidelines, he felt shaken and unprotected, knowing the distracted cars could mow him down as he straggled across the parking lot to a bench in front of the frozen yogurt shop. "Yolo," it was called. "You only live once." He knew what that meant but wondered if the people rushing around him knew.

Without the Mustang as his armour and muscle, and on foot, he was slow. He paused in the middle of the parking lot. The bustle and hurry of everyone in their recent-model cars boiled around him, the traffic on the access roads churning and the preoccupied drivers' eyes passing over him as if he was just some kind of a relic, coming between the past and now, their pressing, rushing, imperious now. He'd been like that, too. He settled onto the bench in the shade, his leg with the capricious knee straight out in front of him, and waited for the tow truck in the glare of sun flashing on mirrors and glass, the hoods of moving cars. Meanwhile, the Barracuda had settled down too, parked and empty outside the Tim Hortons.

He'd have to make it back across the parking lot because his Mustang was over there. He'd have to catch a ride back to his son's house with the tow truck. He knew how it would be. He'd get a boost up into the seat and sit beside the driver, returning to the empty spot in his son's garage. What if it drove away without him, the Mustang disappearing like an empty shell being hauled away without its soul, not just because it wouldn't start but because he was standing outside it, watching it go.

Why couldn't it always be the way it was on Saturday nights when the past gathered, recreating itself out of restored paint, updated engine parts, and polished, exotic chrome, while the spectators strolled amongst them? He dozed a bit, in the heat.

They'd show off and talk for a while, get some frozen yogurt like they used to get ice cream at the drive-in, cruising the small towns of their youth, wander around and compare cars, then when the sun got low, crawl back into them like donning a new body, whole, revived and fully functioning again. Their companions, no longer the young and expectant girls of the past, slid into the passenger side, perched on the old bench seats for the respectable ride home again instead of out to park at the bush or the beach to mess around in the expanses of leather seats hidden by steamed, manually rolled-up windows.

He thought of her in the Barracuda, with her grey hair pulled back in a ponytail, coming here with the survivor car but never lined up with the rest of them. Her car had not only the original turquoise colour, but the actual original paint, bridging the patches of rust. His Mustang had been like that once, before he spent all those hours, while he still could, sanding and filling, getting rid of the weakness, disguising the depredations of life and time, making her new and pretty again. Unlike the perfect, restored surface of his Mustang, the Barracuda's paint was matte and worn, its surface reflecting nothing whatsoever, just absorbing sun on a day like this, smug in its long, life-roughened, event-wrinkled past. It sure didn't blind you just to look at it like some of the restored muscle cars.

Her car might someday be restored, but he doubted it, remembering the tanned, creased skin of her throat and upper chest, the flesh leading from her neck down to the startling whiteness of her shirt. Her skin, he thought, like the faded metal of the Barracuda, would be sun-warmed and salty from sweat, and you could probably taste the wind off the ocean that flew over her while she gunned it down the highway toward the beach. He thought of the hot summer days and nights when they were all young. Her skin could never again be like the glistening, unmarked paint, but was weathered like the Barracuda, baring its unnoticed secrets in tiny seductive wrinkles. He almost closed his eyes, sitting there in the sun, waiting for the tow truck, when he saw it arrive. At the same time, she came out of the coffee shop to her car.

The truck pulled up to his Mustang, and its harried driver, come to rescue him, hopped out and set to work after a brief wave to him across the lot. This guy knew exactly what to do.

He'd dealt with him before. By the time he made his way back, it was almost ready to go, resting there, secured, but with no power, no choice, dependant on the bar, ready to be dragged away.

"Where do you want it?" the guy asked, so he gave his son's address and hesitated while the driver paused to see if he needed help getting up into the passenger side of the truck.

While he stood there, the Barracuda, still burning oil, came up alongside. She pulled in close to him, and he could look down into her eyes that matched the faded blue paint of the car itself. Her window was rolled down. There was no air conditioning in it, he knew, and he could feel the heat rising up to him from inside, and it smelled like the interior had been closed up for years then opened like a door to the past.

"Like a ride?"

He looked down at her, saw two bottles of Coke resting on the console. He glanced into the faint, sly suggestion beyond the top button of her shirt: that old and weathered skin, salty, he'd bet, from sweat and the beating sun and wind from driving the highway on a day like this.

He could smell the exhaust burning, curling around his legs while the engine growled and waited for his answer.

He considered the tow truck driver, who was already turning back to his truck. "You just drop it off there. I'll get a ride." And he made his way around to the passenger side, opening the door, feeling it creak like his knee did more and more these days, feeling its old-fashioned weight, like the door on his Mustang. He eased himself down and into her worn and comforting depths.

He didn't know her name, but a long stream of exhaust would trail them as they took the highway, he and the metal and rubber and glass, the oil and the gas. And the woman. He climbed in and felt his knee start to relax. He would learn her name soon enough, as it was written in the fumes left behind them like a burnt bridge, taunting the ones on the other side. "Here," she said. "I got you a cold drink. Let's go sit by the ocean and watch the boats. I know a place where it's not too hot but still in the sun."

SiWC 2018
October 19-21
+ master classes Oct 18

@SiWCtweets

registration opens on **June 6, 2018**
www.siwc.ca for details

THE BUMBLEBEE FLASH FICTION CONTEST

THE BUMBLEBEE FLASH FICTION CONTEST

Every year, *Pulp Literature*'s summer issue is invigorated with the buzz of a flash fiction champion. Contest judge Bob Thurber crowned RS Wynn queen bee with her story, 'Lullaby, Valentine, Paper Crane'. About the story, he has this to say:

Such a neatly crafted package, wicked fun to read. Consisting of five animated portraits with a small cast of quickly drawn characters frozen in familiar and alarming poses, it spills across the page, causes one to blink, and question, and remember. Like any good short work, poetry or prose, it's a joy to reread just to appreciate the fresh flavor all over again. — Bob Thurber

Alex Reece Abbott's short story, 'Alphabet Soup', received an honorable mention for its sharp sting as well, and will appear in the Autumn 2018 issue. To everyone who submitted their flash fiction, we thank you for your commitment to the craft and hope to see you next year!

The 2018 Bumblebee Flash Fiction Contest Shortlist
'Alphabet Soup' by Alex Reece Abbott
'Breaking the Ice' by Natalie Persoglio
'Cinnamon Grace' by Jude Neale
'Crow Funeral' by Alex Reece Abbott
'Far from the Madding Crowd' by KW George
'Gross Motor' by Sara Mang

'Inciting Insight' by Soramimi Hanarejima
'Special People' by Alex Reece Abbott
'Lullaby, Valentine, Paper Crane' by RS Wynn
'Third Date' by Nicole Vuong

RS Wynn lives in Maine in an antique farmhouse, which she shares with her family and the perfect number of dogs (four, in case you were wondering). She earned an MFA in Writing from Vermont College of Fine Arts. Her short fiction won Pithead Chapel's 2017 Larry Brown Short Story Award, and she has an essay forthcoming in Inscape.

In writing 'Lullaby, Valentine, Paper Crane', she wanted to explore the odd ways in which adult relationship dynamics take root in childhood. As a daughter and step-parent, she is mindful that loving intentions can sometimes be ciphered by children into strange code. These interpreted lessons go where they go, and the results may surprise, amuse, or alarm.

LULLABY, VALENTINE, PAPER CRANE
BY RS WYNN

I.

I remember Marybeth's open-mouthed sobbing, tears coursing down marshmallow cheeks and rounding her chin. A stream flowed from the nook between her legs, too, darkening the tan loop carpet in Mrs Serles's third grade classroom. I remember the odour of Marybeth's urine, whisper sweet, like warm bread, but sharper—if a scent could cut you. At home, my mother sang when she changed my brother's diapers, "Hush-a-bye, don't you cry," but no one sang to Marybeth; we laughed at her. We turned on 'Stinky Mary', on 'Little Bo-Peed'. We all knew the menace of erasure, and all thought, "Thank God it wasn't me!" as Brian swatted the air, and Richard held his nose, and Lauren shrieked. And I — I bloated with laughter. But then Mrs Serles started crying, too. How many years, how many years had she given to children so petty and cruel?

II.

One lunch, Dena traded her Gushers for Amy's Fruit Roll-Up and her bologna sandwich for Brian's turkey and cheese. My lunch — chunky peanut butter (salt and sugar free) brushed lightly on whole wheat, and a raspberry yogurt that was ninety percent seeds — was useless to me in this bartering economy. Sometimes my mother packed a string cheese, not good enough to trade but at least not an embarrassment to me. She said a wholesome lunch showed how much she loved me, and I suppose the stony Grape Nuts she poured for me each breakfast meant the same. I forced it all down; I knew my debt for her love was an immaculate plate. Sometimes I wished my mother loved me less, though, like Dena's parents or like Amy's. Love, I learned, is synonymous with discomfort. It tastes like a punishment. It hurts your teeth.

III.

Karlie ate glue and wore sweatpants from Walmart. I can't say which damned her more in our eyes. And her hair (dirty blonde, I'd heard someone call it) was as greasy as leftover lunchbox cheese; it had that curdled kind of stink. I remember Valentine's

Day in fourth grade. All the girls looked their prettiest, and even Karlie's hair was clean. We traded cards before recess, aching to bestow our Sweethearts meaningfully: *Be Mine, Sugar Pie. Ask Me.* Karlie saved her best for Brooks Darling: a pink pair of confections begging *Kiss Me, Marry Me.* Brooks ate her confession without reading. He signed his valentines coolly, *From B*—all except the one he gave me, which he signed in red marker, *Love You, B.* I saw Karlie alone on the swings next recess, her hair-strings flying, pumping her feet. She eyed me from a floating height.

IV.

One recess, I remember, Lauren and I decided to be bullies. We let Amy in on our plan, too, as it required a third. Ice smothered the schoolyard. Other girls and boys padded by in snow pants, skittering across the wastes, or slowly spun in circles, opening their arms to the frozen-over sky. But we three, Lauren and Amy and I, hooked our arms together and charged straight across the ice. Amy was our plow, levelling enemies in our path. Down went Richard, who'd pull out my hair to floss his teeth. Down went Brian, who'd pinch me and flee into the boy's bathroom. Down went Andy too, who'd always been nice but was in the wrong place at the wrong time. "The Bruised, Battered Friends" we called ourselves, pledging eternal amity. And I learned, even then, to stay safe within a secret, to trade bruises for a vow.

V.

In fifth grade, Karlie moved away. No one asked where she'd gone. Girls disappeared sometimes. We'd all seen the sort of news our parents watched on TV. You must be vigilant, grown-ups said, and I knew why. I'd seen how girls disappeared: they folded into themselves like paper cranes with sharp edges and — gone! They bowed their heads crying, like Marybeth, and were never heard from again. On the news, girls disappeared in cities, they vanished from grocery stores and parking lots, but I'd seen them disappear from a cafeteria and playground just as easily. I'd seen them vanish from a classroom without a sound. On the news, girls sometimes drowned alone in lakes and rivers, but I'd seen them drown in a crowd. If she's lucky, maybe Karlie will drown in love — someday. When her body is swept away, I think she'll sigh with relief.

BLUE SKIES OVER NINE ISLES

Joseph Stilwell and
Hugh Henderson

Joseph Stilwell has slain gods, devoured galaxies, and sired several ruling dynasties. He is either the most powerful man in the multiverse, or a very accomplished liar. See more of his lies @animisticengine on Twitter.

Hugh Henderson is a Vancouver-based artist who is doing a terrible job convincing himself that he knows what he is doing. His passion for science fiction has inspired much of the design of Blue Skies Over Nine Isles, and he has been constructing and refining the visual landscape of the comic for over five years.

In the first chapter of the post-post-apocalyptic Blue Skies Over Nine Isles (Pulp Literature Issue 14, Spring 2017), escaped prisoner Max Romero goes from frying pan to fire when he finds his aircraft short a fuse and himself at the wrong end of a weapon . . .

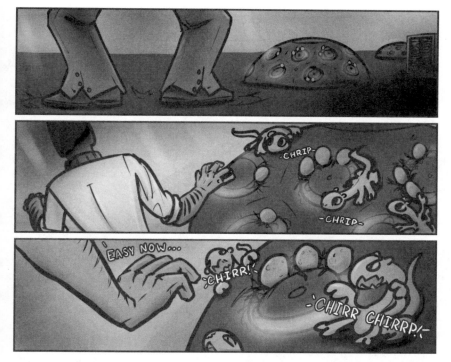

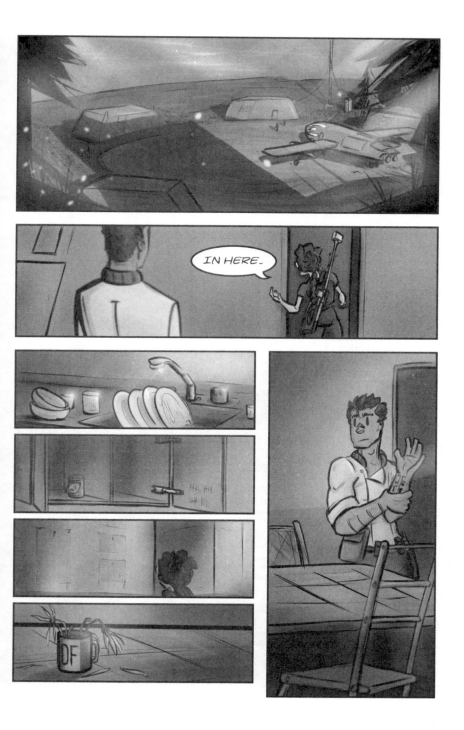

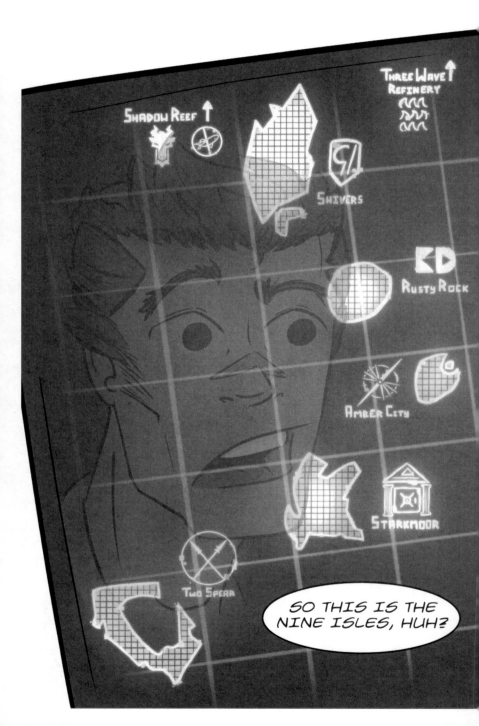

TO BE CONTINUED....

ALLAIGNA'S SONG: ARIA

JM Landels

Allaigna's Song: Aria *is the second novel in the Allaigna's Song trilogy by equestrian swordswoman, artist, and editor* **JM Landels**. *The first book,* Overture, *is available from Pulp Literature Press. You can follow JM's adventures with pen and sword at jmlandels.stiffbunnies.com.*

$\mathscr{P}$REVIOUSLY IN ALLAIGNA'S SONG ...

Fleeing an unwanted betrothal and enraged by her family's lies concerning her parenthood, fourteen-year-old Allaigna has set off to find her true father. However, her quest is interrupted a mere three days in when a chance encounter lands her in the illegal poaching encampment of her betrothed-to-be, Tiern Doniver. She is recognized but escapes, only to be brought in by Morran Rhoan, a travelling singer in the employ of Doniver.

Trapped by thinly veiled threats, she is forced to remain at White Tooth in the guise of an apprentice. However, when a drunken Doniver decides to claim his promised bride, Allaigna's ability to create magic from music takes a deadly turn, killing her betrothed captor.

VERSE 11
FUGITIVE

Morran was in the stables as promised, with Nag saddled, my bags packed, and the change of clothes laid out for me.

The shaking arms and legs that had propelled me down the back stairs of Doniver's tower suddenly gave way, and I hit the floor of Nag's stall, retching into the straw bedding.

"What, too much wine?"

Rhoan's bemused voice filtered into my head, the first words I'd truly heard since I fled the tower room.

"Did your song not work, and you had to drink him under the table?" Rhoan continued. "I'm surprised you can still walk, girl.

"Lass ..." his hand fell on my back, patting uneasily. "Are you all right? Did he —"

"He's dead," I gasped out, and vomited again.

There were some more unanswered questions from Rhoan while I continued to squeeze my now empty stomach dry.

Finally he handed me a stable rubber and a canteen. I sat on my haunches, trembling, wiping my face, trying to stomach the water, trying to make the words come out properly.

"He's dead, Morran," I said in a voice flat enough to squash the terror. "I killed him." The last came out in a whisper, and helpless tears started.

Rhoan took me in his arms. I tensed, nearly convulsed again as I recalled the dead man in whose arms I'd been only minutes before. But Rhoan's embrace was brotherly ... fatherly, even. I shuddered, breathed, and let him shield me from the world with his arms while I told him what happened.

It seemed like an age we sat there in the straw, me sobbing into his chest. But it was probably only a few minutes. The implications of what I'd done began to outweigh the sheer horror of it, and I pushed myself to my feet.

I began stuffing my change of clothes into Nag's saddlebags. I'd have to ride in the dress—there was no time to change.

"I've got to go now," I said. "It won't be long ... before ... before someone finds him."

Morran caught my wrist and I flinched, feeling Doniver's grip once more.

"You can't leave. Not now!" His whisper was hoarse.

I began to struggle, panicking again.

"Sh, sh, sh. Stop, lass! Think!" His hands were gentle once more, holding both mine as if they flowers. "If you disappear now, everyone will know it was you. Who saw you?"

"A ... a serving girl."

"And did she recognize you—Nalen, my apprentice?"

I paused and looked down at the borrowed blue and grey finery.

"Probably not," I admitted.

"And if she did recognize you, it is her word against yours. And mine. And I, for one, know you spent the evening restringing my harp."

He put a gentle hand under my chin, and I flinched like a head-shy foal. Why did he have to do the same things as Doniver ... and yet so differently?

"Can you manage to maintain that story?"

I nodded. Avoiding the truth wasn't hard. But to stay here, after what I'd done ... The urge to flee was strong enough to set my whole body shivering.

He must have seen it in my eyes. "I will get you safely away, lass. I promised, and I'll keep that promise. It will just be later than we planned. But easier too. After all, what is keeping us here?"

The realization was yet another cold shock to the stomach. Indeed, the man who'd kept me here was dead. And he'd given me an identity that would allow me to simply walk away.

Morran interrupted my sudden relief. "There will be an inquiry, of course. No one will be allowed to leave the keep for a while. But after they conclude he was killed by one of his many courtesans—"

My self-interest wavered. "I don't want one of them accused."

He gave a twitch of his mouth. "Not to worry, lass. The courtesan who did this, I think they'll find, already disappeared mysteriously.

"Now change out of that soiled dress and get back to work on my harp strings." He waved long fingers at the chaos of Nag's stall and the patiently waiting horse. "I'll deal with this."

Sure enough, the blue and grey dress turned up several days later, torn, soaked with blood, and buried in a midden heap. Rumours circulated under the masterful, invisible hand of Morran Rhoan, caulking together a tale of a pair of travelling entertainers, husband and wife, who had applied to the castle for a commission. It was amazing to watch Rhoan work. He would approach a guard or a porter, saying, "Do you recall the fair travelling singer? The one with hair as rich as polished bronze and eyes like pools of amber ale?" His rapturous description of the imaginary woman and her matching, very real dress soon had the listener convinced he remembered her and her silent, dark husband. All manner of varied speculation would take wing from there, with no further prompt from Rhoan.

So pervasive were the rumours I could almost convince myself to believe them. At least when others were around. In private, or with Rhoan, my only ally, accomplice, and perhaps friend, I writhed in an agony of despair and self-loathing over the murder I had committed. I allowed myself to crumple with the weight of guilt, emptying my stomach at least every night into the chamber pot. Each time, Morran would hand me a cloth and water and, in a patient drill, I would drink, waiting for the inevitable headache to come. Just punishment, I knew, for my crime.

"It's ..." he began one night.

"I know," I snapped. "It's all right. No one will connect me to the deed." *I see that. I see how right and clever you've been.* "But maybe I deserve to be ... to be ..."

"Implicated? Accused? Tried? Hanged?" I flinched at each word, gentle as they were in his slow, drawling voice. "How often must I remind you, you were defending yourself?"

"He wouldn't have killed me. I should have just ..."

"Let him rape you?"

The word grated like a knife in my already aching head, and I retched, ready to empty my stomach again.

"I would have lived," I said between clenched teeth, holding back nausea.

"And I would have killed him anyway."

He said this with such dark measure in his normally easy voice it took my breath away. I felt at once flattered, protected, and uneasy. I wanted no attachment, no father figure save the one, the true one, for whom I searched.

I shook my head. "No. I would have." It was probably a lie. Would I have taken revenge with a knife or sword? Strange that the thought repelled me less than the murder I had actually done. If I'd killed him with the sword alone, that I could comprehend. But that my voice, so unintentionally, so easily, could steal a life — I could not come to grips with that.

My face was wet with tears.

"Look at me," I snapped, wiping my face. "I make a terrible boy."

Rhoan handed me a lace-edged handkerchief. "Boys cry. Especially when they kill a man for the first time."

"Have you ever ..." I couldn't finish the sentence.

He looked at the floor, shook his head. "No," he said softly.

"Then what do you know about it!" I hissed at him.

I balled up the handkerchief and threw it at the hearth.

It fell short of the flames, and lay there, crumpled and drying. I stomped off to the sleeping area and threw myself onto my trundle bed, not bothering to undress.

Rhoan stayed where he was, but I could hear him pick up his harp and begin to tune it.

"Rhoan?" I asked at last, my voice weak and timid.

"Mm?" he asked.

"Play something."

The tune was not one I knew, but it was oddly familiar. There was a Leisanmira lilt to the phrasing and a resonance in the bone that both thrilled and comforted. My headache was too fierce for me to hear the words, but they left half-conscious images within my brain as I fell asleep, clutching the fine bright flowers of my eversweet posy.

I dreamed of my mother that night, and of my true father.

Verse 12

The Lost Bride

When I awoke before the cockerel I couldn't sort my dream from the tangle of words Rhoan had left lying in my head.

I used the pot, dressed, washed my face, and then paced the chamber until my fretting steps caused a stirring from behind the bed-curtain that contained Rhoan. Since the death of Tiern Doniver the keep had been in mourning and there was no call for musicians in the evening. This by itself kept Rhoan's drinking down, as did a prudent need to keep a wise head and a close tongue. But hung over or not, Rhoan was not a morning person, and his waking was slow and owl-like.

"Sing it to me again," I demanded when he at last emerged.

"What?" he mumbled.

"The one you sang last night. 'The Lost Bride'. No ... don't sing it." I still hadn't stopped pacing and his owlish stare followed me around the room. "Just tell me the words."

"What, now?" he yawned.

I stared him down until he began:

"*Fierce winter frost still gripped the ground,*
The air was bright and sere
When from the crownèd Bastion hill
Rode forth the princess fair."

I shook my hand at him, as if waving off midges. "No, never mind, not the words," I said, though that was what I'd demanded. "Just give me the plot."

"I can't believe you've never heard it," he said grumpily, dropping the coverlet that still rested on his shoulders and moving to the basin to wash his sleep-disordered hair. "Where did you say you grew up?"

"I didn't," I snapped, burning with impatience that quickened my pacing to a near trot. "The plot. Please?"

He yawned again, wiping his face dry. "Princess sets forth on a journey to marry her beloved, is captured by bandits, rescued by faeries, and lives as one of them for fourteen years before returning from the Otherland, nary a day older than when she left. He, now twice her age, sets aside the wife he took in her stead and weds his true love, ending the war between their countries."

My pacing had stopped and I sank into Rhoan's usual chair by the hearth. "Not fourteen years — a fortnight," I whisper to myself. "And not the Otherland." I look accusingly at Rhoan. "The Greatwood. Not faeries. Ilvani."

He raised his eyebrows. "Most ballads, even the fantastical ones, have a grain of truth."

"The bride," I say. "She's Lauresa of Brandishear." *My mother.* I stop myself from saying it out loud.

My eventual reprieve from the White Tooth, scene of my crime, was as prosaic as my first attempted escape was catastrophic.

Morran came whistling into the apartment. "Pack your bags, lad. Again." He grinned.

I jumped to my feet, alarm coursing through my body.

"What is it?" My voice croaked as it came out. I couldn't trust the verity of his smile. "Am I found out?"

He laughed, swept his arms around me and scooped me off the floor, kissing the top of my head. "Not a bit of it. Breathe easy, lass."

He put me down, ruffling my hair with a familiarity that annoyed me far more than the hug or kiss. I backed away, smoothing it down and straightening my shirt, exasperated.

"Well tell me, then!"

He was still grinning. "I'll tell you, lass, I've never been so happy to be let go."

"You mean you've been dismissed?"

"We, lass. *We've* been dismissed. Young Tiern Doniver was my patron, not his father. It seems House Doniver has no need of entertainments, especially in this period of mourning."

The sick guilt that twisted my stomach at every mention of my former betrothed now torqued even harder, knowing I'd cost Rhoan his commission as well, and choked any relief I felt.

"And further," Rhoan continued with unwarranted cheerfulness, "House Doniver's treasury is a bit lean at the moment. It seems young Doniver made more than a few investments that haven't yet paid off—"

"And won't," I spat, the guilt lifting for the space of a breath as I thought of the cruel beast-baiting project I'd foiled.

"Oh, that wasn't Tiern Doniver's only illicit venture," said Rhoan, guessing my thoughts. "Whether you intended to or not, you've done your father a great service by disposing of a considerable thorn in his side."

My first blinding thought was fury that he would marry me to such a thorn. My second, falling over that immediately, was,

"My fath ... " I gasped, open-mouthed. "How ... who do you think my father is? Did *he*," I said, meaning Doniver, "tell you?"

Rhoan was busy packing his things. "I'm a troubadour, Allaigna." I jerked at the use of my name, glancing at the open door to our chambers. He kept his voice low. "I'm used to taking small bits of information and stringing them into a story. It didn't take much to guess your identity. And," he added, "just because I make fast work of guesses doesn't mean others can't follow my thoughts. Which is why I'd say you've lingered overlong in Aerach. If escaping your family is truly your wish."

Was it still? I thought. I no longer had an unwanted betrothal to run from. But that wasn't the real reason I'd left home. It was the lies, the layers and tangled strands of them, twisted about me since childhood, that I could no longer support.

"It is," I said. "I've been packed forever. Shall we go?"

I have taken other lives — too many others — since Tiern Doniver's. Some were more deserving of death, perhaps. Others less. But who am I to judge? I cannot peer into the minds of others and see what actions come from malice and what are true regrets. I cannot see the hidden good or ill many might have done, nor can I scry the future like my grandmother and see what consequence may befall this deed or that.

But no other death haunts me as Tiern Doniver's has. I did not mean to kill him — had no idea my voice could even do that. But, as my grandmother would have said, ignorance is the coward's excuse. I should have known. I should have stayed at home where Angeley could have schooled my voice further. I could have taken the geas never to use magic upon another — and after Doniver's murder I nearly did — or simply used my wits rather than my unproven, unharnessed gipsy magic. I have many regrets, and many deaths upon my head, but this one remains the greatest.

VERSE 13

Hiding in Plain Sight

We had been on the road together less than a day, Morran Rhoan and I, before we had our first argument.

"Absolutely not!" I pulled Nag up hard, causing him to toss his head in annoyance.

Rhoan turned, leaned a hand on his cantle, but didn't slow his bay mare's walk.

"The sun's getting low, lass. The Bend and Bow's a fine inn, but the best beds will be gone soon."

I would have yelled back at him not to call me 'lass', but an ox cart had appeared at the turn in the road ahead, and a loud discussion on my sex and identity was out of the question.

Nag fidgeted and danced, impatient to catch up with the other horse, but I stubbornly held him in place, spinning small circles on the muddy road while Rhoan made a resigned turn back to us.

"Be reasonable, lass—"

"Lad!" I hissed, now he was close enough again.

He let his laconic gaze roll up and down me, and sighed heavily.

"Have it your way ... lad," he said. "But a girl posing as a boy is bound to draw more questioning looks than simply a girl."

"Are you saying I can't pass as a boy?" I scowled contemptuously at him. Of course I could. I still had no chest to speak of, and I had the build of a ten-year-old boy, not a fourteen-year-old girl.

There was a sad little quirk at the corner of his mouth. "Maybe," he said without sounding like he believed it. "Until you speak."

"What's wrong with my voice," I growled, lowering it. "I can talk like a boy."

He laughed. "A boy your size has the voice of a reed pipe, my dear. You've a lot to learn about disguise and misdirection before I can put you in front of the public like that."

"Which is why we are *not* going into that town!"

The ox cart was rumbling nearer, and I nudged my horse off the road to let it pass. Our conversation halted for the long slow minutes it took the beasts to trundle past. Nag was fully agitated now, as was the bard's horse, by our lack of forward momentum.

The drover gave me a friendly smile and wave as he moved past, calling out to Rhoan. "That's a fell beast you've mounted that wee slip of girl on, sir. Red Anders at the east side of the village has some nice cobs in his stable. He's an honest trader—ye'd make a fine deal."

Rhoan lifted his hat. "Thank you, good sir! Most grateful indeed."

He said nothing to me as he waved the drover off, but the expression on his face was insufferable.

"*That* is why we're going nowhere near any towns," I spat when the cart was far enough away.

"Don't be absurd, Allaigna." He used my name just to irritate me, I was sure. "Look at the sky. We're in for another soaking like we had this morning, only this time with no sunshine to dry us off. I'm still damp and have no intention of getting damper when there's a perfectly good inn just over the hill there, with a fire, hot food, and a mattress with only a few fleas in it."

"You've seen yourself—in fact you've been at pains to point out—just how inadequate my disguise is, and you want me to go into a village?"

"As a boy, no. As my daughter, I think it's perfectly plausible."

"As ... your ... daughter?"

He bowed from the saddle. "I know my humble origins don't match your noble bloodlines, but really, do we look so different?"

His hair was wavy, but as black as mine. His eyes were brown, not grey, but his build was thin and gangly: much more similar to mine than Allenis Andreg's was. In fact, he looked more like me than either of my parents did.

He caught my wondering look. "No. I'm not. Really. But it's not such an implausible thing, is it?"

I followed him down the muddy road to the village, devastated by the tiny moment of hope that had dashed through my heart and fled.

It was in fact easy for Rhoan to pass me off as his daughter, Merry. As Morran and Merry we sang for board that night. The strain of singing ordinary notes and words, letting no hint of magic creep into my voice, made me hoarse and tense. If it hadn't been for Morran's practised ease, I'm sure we would have earned no bed at all.

I hadn't sung since the night I'd killed a man with my voice, and the terror of it strung my nerves tighter than Rhoan's harp strings. By the end of the evening my head throbbed with the worst headache yet. I fell into bed without eating the supper for which I'd sung, and spent the night with my dreams of terrified guilt and the empty eyes of Tiern Doniver.

My head still pounded when I awoke, and Morran couldn't drag me from bed till well past the breakfast hour.

"Faith, lass, if this is your aspect after a single mug of watered cider, I'd hate to see you recover from a real drunk."

I growled something unintelligible at him and filled my stomach with prunes and water, not daring to brave the noise of the tavern below for warm porridge. We packed our saddlebags in silence, till at last Rhoan cleared his throat and tossed a handful of bronze and silver coins onto the bed.

"Not too bad a turning for last night, it seems."

I looked at the coins in puzzlement, unable to comprehend.

"That's from the punters," he explained. "They liked us enough to throw some extra coin our way. That's your share."

I thought about refusing it. I hardly felt I'd earned it. But I was in no position to be turning down silver. The metallic clink of the money as I dropped it in my pouch sounded like the snip of scissors ... or knives. It was ominous, but liberating. It had been over a month since I'd left home, but only now did I feel free of it.

It was, as Rhoan had promised, a fairly good inn. But the horses' accommodation was better than ours. Each of our mounts was bedded down in a roomy box with a generous layer of straw on the floor and good hay in the manger. I relaxed as I entered the stable. My gut, knotted since we'd left Doniver or even since I'd left home, unclenched at last in the soothing beams of the thick morning sun.

Which is why I was completely off-guard when, after opening the bottom half of Nag's stall door, I was bowled over backward by a pair of grizzled paws planted on my chest.

It only took a fraction of a panicked second to realize the creature, a large gazehound, was not snarling but smiling his wet, slobbery grin, tongue out, dog breath filling up my face. As I heaved the beast's paws off me I recognized it.

"Dog!" I exclaimed, not at the beast but at its master, who also stuck his straw-coloured head out from under the top door. "What are you doing here?"

Not that he could answer me any more than I could understand his tongue-less clicks and whistles. The bitch sat politely behind her master, thumping her tail on the ground, while her mate busily circled me, sniffing my boots and legs.

"Is Raddick here?" I asked, half-hoping he wasn't — that he was settled back at his family's farm.

But sure enough, up out of the manger popped a sleepy, hay-prickled head.

"Did someone say my name? Mistress Merry!" He scrambled out of the manger, tripping as he did, and threw himself on bended knee at my feet. "It's so ... so very good to see you safe, my lady Merry!"

His head was lowered, but I could tell from the bright pink tips of his ears he was blushing. Nag, who still hadn't received his morning grain, was indifferent to all this human and canine traffic in his stall. He gave me an impatient nudge with his head, sending me tripping over Raddick to the embarrassment of us both.

"Get up, Raddick," I snapped, sounding like Angeley. "There's no room in here for courtesy. What are you doing here?"

Rhoan, who had been settling the account with the landlord, appeared at this moment and stuck his head under the stall door.

"A party! And no one asked me!" he exclaimed. "Why, 'tis

the little lad to whom you had me deliver those deeds. Boy, you scarcely look better now than when you were living rough — did you not reclaim your farm?"

Raddick was hastily straightening his tunic and picking chaff from his hair. "No, sir ... I mean yes, sir. The farm is mine in name and deed, thanking your good selves."

"Oh, the lady Ah ..." He paused. "The lady Merry here, she did all the work. I was just the errand boy."

I frowned. "If you got the farm back, why are you here?"

"Well." He shrugged. "Um ... It seems your, uh, intervention gave me more than my ma ever had, like. Y'see, we were leaseholders before. The deeds you sent were for a freehold."

"Yes, I know." I was rather proud of that, negotiating more from Doniver than Raddick had ever had.

"Well, so, I can't farm that much land on my own ... and it didn't seem right to toss out the farmer and 'is family of seven who work the land now."

"So you're a homeless landlord, is that it?" laughed Rhoan.

He nodded, blushing again. "They're building a new house for me in exchange for this year's rents ... but until it's finished, well, Dog and I have nowhere to live."

"So you've come to ask another favour of the lady who's bettered you already," said Rhoan in his sternest voice. I knew he was mocking, but Raddick shook in his boots.

"No, sir. Of course not, sir. It's just ..." He turned to me, pleading, and dropped to one knee again, narrowly missing one of Nag's piles of droppings. "I swore my oath to you, lady — that hasn't changed. And since I've naught to do on my lands ... well, I thought I'd be of service, like."

It was my turn to be embarrassed now. I looked at Rhoan.

"Didn't you convey the whole message? I released him from his oath."

Rhoan looked amused. "It seems, lady Merry, the young swain has declined to take it back. That's his prerogative, I'm afraid."

"Raddick, I ... Oh, Fingal's balls!" I swore. "I'm flattered. Truly. It's just ... we're travelling fast and light, Rhoan and I." I looked over to him for cues, but he was impassive, and still amused, damn him. "We haven't any other horses, and——"

"Oh, m'lady, I did not expect to *accompany* you!"

I breathed my relief.

"Though it would be an honour beyond my worth." He looked at me with those giant hazel eyes, reminding me more and more of the two hounds also staring me down. "I merely came to see if I can do you some boon."

Dog gave a series of quiet clicks, and Raddick jumped.

"Oh ... I nearly forgot!" he pulled a crumpled handbill from his shirt and passed it to me. "I can't read it, of course, but it looks like ..."

And of course it was: cleaner-looking than I was now, but unmistakably me.

Why now? I wondered. Why had it taken so long for my family to start papering the countryside with my face?

Rhoan looked genuinely sad when he saw the handbill. "Your parents must be desperate with worry, Allaigna. Would it not be better to simply return home? Your fiancé is no longer ... a concern. What have you to fear?"

Fear? Nothing. Not even my parents' or Angeley's anger would give me pause. Pride—now that was another thing. And anger. The anger was still there.

"Oh yes, Doniver's gone. But I'm sure they've notified the next on a very long line of suitors already."

And then I realized why the handbills had appeared only now. They had thought I was safe at Doniver—he had broken his word, no doubt—and I almost wondered if they'd been depending on him to keep me there.

Fury boiled up inside me again, as fresh and new as it had been that early morning I'd left home.

But Rhoan persisted, insisted that I at least send word. And so I wrote a letter on the back of the handbill, to Mother—not Angeley or Father—informing her of my good health and my lack of intention to return home. Also instructing her to reward the messenger well.

Dog, being both unlettered and mute, could not be questioned, making him the perfect messenger. I would have sent Raddick with him, at least as far as Teillai city, but Rhoan had other advice.

"Lad, your tenants may be glad to be no longer beholden to Doniver, but that makes them anomalies in their neighbourhood. You would do well to maintain a presence. Rent a room in town, do odd jobs for your keep, but visit your farm regularly. And if you can't afford a horse, hire one and learn to ride it when you inspect your farm. No matter how good your tenants may be, you are now their landlord, and they need to be reminded of it."

So easily, I thought, a careless word of mine had changed Raddick from peasant to gentry, and thrown the responsibility of land onto his shoulders. Would he thank me for it? Would he rise to his new station, or be forever outcast, a true member of neither class? That sense of responsibility almost did make me want to take him along. To relieve him of his duties, and take him under my wing. I could tell he would jump at the chance. But my wing was too thin and frail to shelter myself, never mind another. The best thing I could do for Raddick was say goodbye to him.

I surprised myself with the depth of my feeling. He had been so loyal, so helpful, so eager to please beyond the debt of the small and questionable service I'd done him. I didn't know how to respond to that sort of fidelity.

"You've changed my life forever, mistress," he said, his wide-set eyes glazed in water. Whatever you need, wherever you need it, you've but to ask. I'm your man." He seemed a bit embarrassed at that last: he was no more a man than I was a woman, and we both knew it. He covered his awkwardness with an attempt at a courtly bow that became even more awkward. I shot a glare at Rhoan, demanding he not laugh. His eyes were merry, but his mouth stayed neutral.

I offered Raddick my hand, wondering if he knew what to do with it and wishing I could teach him the courtly skills I'd learned at Rheran. He did know what to do, though he did it as awkwardly as all else, taking my fingers and kissing them rather too firmly and too long. No, I decided, he wasn't a courtier, and I wouldn't want him to be.

I raised him up and wrapped my arms around him. It felt odd, and I was as awkward as he, embracing someone my own age. I allowed hugs, reluctantly, from my mother and grandmother, but never gave them. This was a gift, pure and simple from my heart to his, and when I broke away I felt, rather than giving, that I had received.

VERSE 14

MISERY

Now that Rhoan had convinced me it was safe to appear in towns, now that the first enticing jingle of coin rattled in my pocket, I was entirely dispirited to have to revert to my original plan of sleeping rough. But the handbills were out there, and even though I cut my hair as short as I could bear (leaving just enough to cover my hated ears), I wouldn't risk being spotted.

I handed Rhoan back my share of the silver from the previous night and demanded he acquire supplies. He did this while I nervously groomed our horses over and over. It was just before noon when he returned with his purchases: a waxed canvas tent, ropes, a new woollen blanket, plenty of flatted and milled oats, salt fish and beef, a large loaf of dark bread, a wheel of cheese, currants, prunes, and a few withered apples and onions that had survived winter storage. To my disapproval he had also bought a skin of wine and a flask of whisky. Since the death of Doniver he'd ceased his evening debauchery, and I had hoped he wouldn't recommence. He assured me it was only to flavour the stews and warm the limbs on cold nights.

"Besides," he added, "a dash of whisky's always good to have for cleaning wounds or numbing the bones. Or making friends. And when you're sleeping rough you need to make friends of all you encounter."

The rain set in when we were only an hour out of Cranhold. By the time we camped for the night, my woollen cloak was soaked through and Rhoan's leather hood and cape were stiff and sodden. In the morning, our clothes were hardly drier, having shared the damp air inside the tent with us. Our boots at least were still dry.

The next few days were even more miserable. The spring rains set in with spite, turning roads to byres, streams to rivers, clothing to sponges, and tempers to bonfires. It was a pity we couldn't warm ourselves on our smouldering, crackling, blazing arguments. Instead we huddled, sodden and chilled, under the only partly waterproof canvas of our tent, chewing on hardtack and jerky, or stomaching cold gruel soaked overnight in the absence of a cooking fire.

Rhoan refused to take his harp out of its case even at night. The air was too moist, he said, and he trusted the oiled and waxed leather more than the soggy canvas above our heads. So we passed the time by singing: ditties, rounds, drinking songs that made me blush, love songs that made me blush even more, and sagas that stirred something deep and restless in me. It was always disquieting when I recognized relatives within a ballad, some as close as Grandpapa, some as distant as Brandis himself, who of course was my great-however-many-greats grandfather. It was odd how I'd always known the facts — that Mother and Grandpapa are descended from the line of Brandis — but I had never made the connection that it is his blood, however many generations diluted, that flows in my veins. Rhoan knew one or two songs about the distant heroes of Aerach, but none of them hooked my imagination as they once might have. Even if they were ancestors of Allenis

Andreg, or his cousin Prince Vishod, I knew now they were no blood of mine.

And then there were the Leisanmira songs: not spell songs, but the ones sung about the campfire. I knew them, for I had heard Angeley sing them many times. But now, knowing they too were part of my blood made me ache with the thrum of those notes.

The only gap in this family history of song forming around me was my father. I asked Rhoan if he knew any Ilvani songs. He cocked his head to one side, as if listening for them in the heavy spatter of rain upon the cloth over our heads.

"I know one or two I can sing by heart. But I only know a few words of Ilvani, so I may not be singing this right."

He launched into a ballad. At least that's what I guessed it was, though the progressions were strange—so full of semitones, minor sixths and seconds—that I had a hard time parsing it. But it vibrated with that same recognition in my bones. Yes, I thought, this must be part of my heritage too.

My Ilvani was a bit better than Rhoan's. Partway through I began to piece together enough lyrics to recognize the plot.

A chill ran through me that had nothing to do with the dampness of my clothes.

"Wait," I said, halting him mid-stanza. "This is about Wellbirk, isn't it?"

He'd sung the familiar, Ilmari version earlier, but this ... this was its mirror. Where the song I knew told of the tragic nobility of High Prince Goffree, my great-grandfather, in the face of insurmountable odds, this one sang of the courage and cleverness of Caradar of House Halobrelia, and how he had defeated the evil tyrant encroaching on the last of the Valnirata lands. I laughed at the cruel irony. All this time spent searching through scarce Ilvani records to learn the other side of the story, and all I really had to was listen to some old songs.

It was no longer so easy to take sides. I didn't know for sure whether my birth father was full Ilvani or a mongrel like me, but in whatever amount, the blood of both peoples mixed uneasily in my veins.

I woke up when cold drops of water from our sodden tent fell onto my head. I heard the sound of water pouring and hoped it was one of the horses relieving itself, rather than Rhoan, so near the tent.

He stuck his head back in. "Wake up, lazy-guts. The rain's stopped for now—as good a time to strike camp as—" He stopped and sniffed. "What's that smell?"

I grimaced. "Don't blame me. I wasn't the one breaking wind all night."

He flicked my toes. "Don't be rude to your elders, little girl. I mean the smell of flowers. I know that scent ... Eversweet."

I sat up, releasing another waft of scent from the posy that hung around my neck.

He inhaled again. "But it doesn't grow here."

I fished the little bundle of herbs out from beneath my shirt. "You mean this?"

His eyes widened. "Where on earth did you get that, lass?"

"I've always had it. Well, since I was little."

"You still are little," he said absently, gently fingering the bundle. "But where did it come from?"

I shrugged and hid it back beneath my shirt. What could I say? From a peasant woman, who was no doubt *not* a peasant woman.

"It was a gift." I was beginning to become irritated by his probing tone. "I've always worn it. You just noticed now?"

"Enclosed air space," he said, tapping the canvas ceiling, causing another shower to fall on my head. He grinned as I scooted backward, knocking my elbow on the tent and wetting it even more. "That must be why I like you. You smell like home."

He moved aside as I crawled out of the tent, shaking my wet head. My boots were still damp, and as I struggled to put them on, hopping on one foot, I used some of Ormé's favourite curses.

"Such a mouth on a high-born lady."

"What do you mean, 'smells like home'?" I growled, before he could mock me any more.

"Well, you must know eversweet grows only on the high mountains in the north of Elalantar? Where the Sîul Ilvani live."

"And you're from the south, like Rhiadne, you said."

"No, I only said I met her there. I grew up west of Ysevan, in the lower slopes of the Bywirn range. My mother used to take me once a year to visit my grandfather's family in the alps. I'm one-sixteenth Ilvani, on my mother's father's mother's side, you know."

"I thought Ilvani didn't breed with Ilmari," I said, trying to sound casual, knowing full well I was proof they did.

"Every rule has its exception, lass. But as far as that goes, you should know the Sîul are less hostile to Ilmari than the Valnirata clans are. They live and trade under Elalantar's rule quite peacefully."

He sounded proud, which made me prickle in defence of my nation and my grandfather, but I suppressed it. I needed to know more about these Ilvani.

"What are they like, the Sîul?"

As we moved about breaking camp, shaking out and rolling up our rain soaked shelter as best as possible, feeding and towelling off the miserable horses, he told me.

They were from the Valnirata originally, exiled long ago. Some say it was for collaborating with Ilmari; some say for intermarrying with them; others say for political reasons that had nothing to do with the Ilmari at all. Most of the Sîul have dark hair unlike their fair-haired cousins, but they still possess the violet eyes and white-pale skin that set them apart from the bronze-skinned Ilmari.

I looked self-consciously down at my own pale wrists, so different from the honey-gold skin of my sisters and mother. Even Rhoan, with his proudly confessed titration of Sîul blood, was far darker-skinned than I.

My mother had told me so little of my father, when she had at last told me anything. He was Ilvani, or at least partly; he had been a squire in Rheran; he had hair and eyes like mine.

I remembered the stranger in the garden the night of my twin sisters' birth feast: the pale cool hand, the thin smile in the narrow white face. I thought of the smell I had noticed then, and realized it had been with me for years. Did the posy come from him? Or the fifth flower that had appeared on that night I'd spent in the Eastern Forest? It was a longing both cold and warm: to be watched over, and cared for; and yet, to be spied upon, shadowed.

And now, certain that my father was Sîul, was there any point pursuing him in the Valnirata Greatwood? Or in Brandishear?

But those were the two places my mother knew him, and it seemed a closer place to start than across the sea in Elalantar.

It took four days in total of cross-country riding to reach the edge of Aerach, three of them spent soaking in the rain, and the fourth spent shivering in the late Ilia wind that dried our clothes but froze us to the bone. By the end of that fourth day, though, I didn't feel the cold, because I was burning from within with the fever that visited me, along with a throat too sore to talk or swallow and legs that ached with every jolting step Nag took.

By late afternoon I no longer noticed the road. It was all I could do to keep my eyes on the rump of Talwis, Rhoan's bay mare, and long before dark descended I'd ceased bothering to keep my eyes open at all. Twice I nearly fell off: the first time jolting awake when my chin hit my chest; the second saved only by some simian reflex that made me clutch Nag's neck as I started to roll out of the saddle.

For all I know, I may have indeed accomplished falling off in the end, for I don't recall anything between that last near miss and waking up in a bed. Not a particularly clean or soft bed, but after soggy, stony, tree-root-ridden ground it might as well have been the softest feather bed in Osthegn.

Alarmed, I sat up like a released trebuchet, making my head swim and pound at the same time. It knocked me back into the bed as quickly as I'd sat up.

My pillow, I noticed as I readjusted to proneness, was Rhoan's velvet-lined jerkin, the one he hadn't worn since we'd left Doniver. My own clothes—just my shirt and breeches—were still damp, but whether from rain or sweat I didn't know. From the mildewy, sour smell that rose from me, I guessed both. The single high window was unglazed and missing a shutter, by grace of which omission a block of chilly daylight relieved the simple room of utter darkness.

I must have slept the entire night, I reasoned, and began

worrying again. We'd agreed to stay out of towns and inns, so why were we here? Had Rhoan decided to ransom me back to my family? Anger warmed me again, and I threw the thin blanket off and struggled to my feet, delusions of complex plots feeding my still-feverish brain. My feet tangled with the blanket and I only just managed to twist my flailing body around to fall on the prickly straw-stuffed mattress rather than the wooden floor, my head now pounding in triple time. The temptation to lie there was too great, and down I stayed till Rhoan came in.

I was confined to the straw-stuffed mattress for the rest of the day and the following night, while Rhoan coddled and fussed over me like a nursemaid. Prickly as the mattress, I resisted at first, trying to dress and vacate the bed every time he left the room; but every time I sat up the blinding headache would slam me back down. By the time he had returned with a midday meal of beef broth, soft bread, and wine-soaked currants, I had resigned myself to my marginally comfortable prison. And once resigned, I relaxed and found the mindless boredom a soothing respite from constant tension.

Since I'd left home — nine weeks, though it seemed a lifetime ago — not a moment had passed without some anxiety twisting through my mind. Even my sleep had been full of worried dreams. I had made friends and enemies, found my life in peril more than once, and caused a death that haunted me. But here, in the dull stillness of the inn room, the cords of tension snapped and released me, and I was able to surrender my care into the kindness of a man I'd known for less than two months.

Strangely, his paternal concern didn't make me long for the father I was seeking, or at least no more than usual. Instead I thought of Mother, and even more of Angeley's cool hands and calm comfort in the face of any illness. At last, I allowed myself to cry for them: not homesick tears of wanting to return, but tears of apology, knowing how much pain I was causing them and wishing in my heart to say sorry. And when I realized I had at last begun to forgive them, there were tears of relief.

Lauresa's Chorus

The long spring dusk has settled over the garden. Nonetheless, she feels exposed. There are many windows that look down into this courtyard from the west hall, the stable loft, the granary and dovecote. But there is one corner that is virtually free of overlook, beneath the plum tree, sheltered from sight lines of the parapets by a buttress flanking a small wooden door. It is no doubt a risk, if a small one, to the defensibility of the castle. Lauresa is convinced it is only by dint of his spending so little time in the courtyard or solar that her husband hasn't noticed. Otherwise, she's sure, he'd order the plum tree Angeley planted when she first arrived cut down.

The dark-cloaked figure is there, as she knew he would be. It has been nearly three years since she's seen him. Then she had two children and another on the way. Now she has twice that number. With each of Andreg's children that she has carried and nursed, she has felt her attachment to the father of her first born grow thin and weak. She senses more than sees him: a veiled piece of darkness revealing no more than a pale chin and knife-like line of a mouth. His breath, warm in the cool night air, is a palpable thing. It erases that thin distance, replacing it with a longing as fresh and strong as the day she first felt it.

A small sound escapes her lips. To call it a moan or a sigh would be to enlarge it beyond its measure. It is a tiny sound, of protest, relief, denial, and surrender, but his sharp ears catch it nonetheless, and he answers not with voice, but with movement. A tiny ripple shivers his cloak like the breath of wind in the plum blossoms.

These two signals, the sound and the movement, are as loud as a shout, stronger than a blow, to their audiences, and for four long liquid heartbeats there is no more sound or movement from either.

"Your Grace," he says at last, just as she reaches a hand towards him, puts her fingers over that thin mouth, and stops any more words.

They are frozen, noiseless, for four more heartbeats before she replaces her fingers with her lips.

It is a long, still kiss, not of passion, but of remembrance. Her body, heavy with a mother's curves, melts into his as if they had never been apart.

"You shouldn't be here," Lauresa says at last. It is stating the obvious, but she has to say something, do something, to prevent herself from dragging him up to her chamber.

"Agreed," he murmurs, his face buried in her hair. He draws in a long, starving breath and releases it, sending warmth through the crown of her head. His arms have not loosened their hold, and she has to curve her spine backward to see his face.

Before she can speak again he stops her with a second kiss, this one more insistent, more urgent than the first. Never mind her chambers: she is in danger of spreading that cloak of his right here in the damp gravel of the garden. His arms become tighter than she thought possible, as if he would crush their bones together, their ribs inextricably tangled and laced like the skeletons found in joint graves, their remains forming the frame for a strange, two-headed, eight-limbed beast. And she would happily perish in that twined embrace. That is, until her breasts, doubly full with the task of feeding two babies, ache and remind her of her other loves, and her other duties.

She lets out a yip of pain and struggles free, adjusting her squashed bosom within her bodice once more.

He steps back with a jerk, the heat of his body replaced by a chill breeze.

"Forgive me, your Grace—I didn't mean to hurt you."

She laughs. "They've seen far worse treatment." The flash of anger that passes over his face makes her laugh again. "From my babies. They've been bitten, grabbed, scratched, elbowed, and even kneeled on." She is babbling, and also giggling like a twelve-year-old at his appalled puzzlement.

She relents, strokes his face, so familiar and yet so forgotten. "You didn't hurt me."

Except with your absence, she adds silently. *And now, your presence.* She is not sure which is worse. Absence is a dull longing, an empty hole in the landscape of her heart that she covers over and steps around, pretending it isn't there. His presence is fire, wounding and delighting. The pain is like a hot southern spice that burns the tongue and upsets the stomach but makes her long for more.

"I am glad you're here," is all she says aloud.

He catches her roaming hand, brings it to his lips, and holds it there as if he would inhale her all, beginning at the fingertips.

"You daughter's voice is exquisite," he says at last.

"Our daughter's."

"You are still sure of that?"

"More and more every day. How did you hear her?"

"Your ... Angeley brought me to the gallery to wait for her."

How thoughtful of her mother, to plant him where he could hear her sing. But ...

"Wait for her?" Einavar was here to see her mother?

"I had news for her—from Brandishear."

It more than irked that he had come all the way here to see Irdaign and not her. Was she just a side visit, then?

He sensed her anger. "It was both urgent and sensitive in the extreme. Believe me, nothing less could induce me to break my word to you and return."

Break his word? Of course. She made him promise not to seek her out again. But that oath, she knew now, was one she'd always in her heart hoped he'd be unable to keep. She pushes away the irritating thought of her mother using her lover as a messenger, determined not to ruin these stolen moments.

"You are forgiven," she says, planting a playful kiss on the bridge of his nose. "But what news is so urgent from Brandishear that my *nurse*"—she spreads deliberate emphasis on the word—"needs it?"

He opens his mouth, closes it again, struggling for the right answer. "I haven't laid eyes on your face or heard your voice in three years. Do we need to talk of that?"

"What else would you talk of?"

"You." He leans forward to kiss her again, but she retreats.

"Me? That's hardly an interesting subject. I have babies; I nurse them, wipe their noses and their bottoms, and toss them like jesters' clubs between my hands and those of my nurses, hoping none of us lets one fall." As she talks, a sharp bitter note edges into her voice. "I order the household, keep records of the number of sacks of rye versus barley in our storehouses, the candles we use and the cost of evenlamps, which barrels of wine and which of ale should be broached each night. It is an army of small details and I am its general. A more boring life you cannot imagine."

He catches her fingers again, tangling them this time in his own. "Then run away with me." He smiles.

The sudden brief thought of it leaves her breathless for a moment, before it slaps her face.

"You cannot be serious," she snaps, then softens her reply. "When you first asked it of me, I wouldn't trade peace in the Ilmar for my own happiness—"

"Are you saying that peace still hangs on this marriage of yours, eight years on?"

She laughs, a sharp humourless sound. "Not in the least. I am utterly unimportant to the current chessboard, I'm sure. And no doubt Allenis would hardly miss me. Or his daughters either, at least until they're of an age to marry. But his son he'd miss, and I would never leave one of my children behind. For anyone."

Einavar looks over her head, up towards the towers of Osthegn. "For that, I could almost hate him."

Hate whom? she wonders. Andreg? Does he not already hate Andreg? She hopes so. But Allenry? He could not possibly mean Allenry, for then she would have to hate Einavar, and her heart couldn't stand that. She doesn't ask for the clarification. Better not to know. This is not the conversation she wants to have.

"What of you? I thought you had rejoined the Rangers."

"I have. I am." He is startled out of his thoughts.

"And yet, here you are." She eyes him, and before he is forced to explain goes on. "One of the loyal Brandishear Rangers my father puts so much faith in. And yet, you really work for my mother."

He lowers his head in acquiescence.

"I work for both. And above all, the Ilmar."

"But what happens when the demands of your masters conflict?"

He doesn't meet her eyes. "They have not, so far."

"So far."

There is another silence. Lauresa feels the weight of his words settle on her. The temptation is so strong to test that loyalty. Find out where his true allegiance lies.

If she were to ask him to reveal her mother's business — ask him directly — would he tell her? Most of her hopes not, and yet the small, childish part of her that wants proof and proof again of his love for her can't help but wish it, ever so slightly.

But she will not test it, not tonight, and perhaps not ever. For she too is beholden to duty.

The euphoria of Einavar's visit lasts nearly a month before the endless stream of bookwork and accounting, the minutiae of mothering five children and a castle full of servants, retainers, and guests pushes down on her shoulders and her feet drag on the solid ground again. Summer's bounty and easy days with children playing in the garden give her some buoyancy, but the suspicion of political undercurrents passing just beneath her nose, and the uneasy feeling her mother knows more about the affairs of her domain than she does, wipes some of the bloom from her happiness. She would delve deeper, try to investigate, if only she had the energy.

She looks back to her time growing up in Rheran and wonders that life was ever so uncomplicated. She wonders too how she could have been so casually oblivious to the politics of court when she had all the time and energy to engage in them. Perhaps if she had been involved, her life would have been different. She might have had a say in whom she married. But then she would not have met Einavar. Allaigna would not be Allaigna, and neither would Allenry, Lauriana, or these two half-sleeping cherubs nestled under her arms, nursing themselves to sleep, their matching fuzzy heads pressed against each other.

Irdina shifts, opens her eyes. Lauresa strokes the bridge of her nose until the blue eyes are hidden again. Branwen stirs as well, eyes still closed, but her tiny hand reaching over towards her sister's face. Lauresa intercepts it before a finger up the nose awakes Irdina. The minute fingers wrap themselves around her long one and both babies settle into a deeper sleep.

No, she would not trade it for anything.

More from Mel Anastasiou

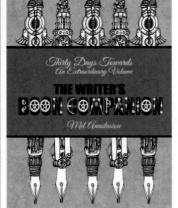

STELLA RYMAN
AND THE FAIRMOUNT
MANOR MYSTERIES

*Longlisted for the 2018
Leacock Medal for Humour*

MEL ANASTASIOU

*Thirty Days Towards
An Extraordinary Volume*

THE WRITER'S
BOOM COMPANION

Mel Anastasiou

at pulpliterature.com

Room magazine's Contest Calendar

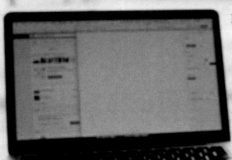

FICTION & POETRY (Apr. 15 - July 15, 2018)
1st Prize: $1000 + publication in Room

SHORT FORMS (Sept. 1 - Nov. 1 , 2018)
1st Prize: $500 + publication in Room

COVER ART (Nov. 15 , 2018 - Jan. 15, 2019)
1st Prize: $500 + publication on cover

Entry Fee: $35 CAD ($42 USD for
International entries). Entry includes a one-year
subscription to *Room*. Additional entries $7.

For more information on our contests
and upcoming calls for submissions,
visit roommagazine.com.

Room
LITERATURE, ART, AND FEMINISM SINCE 1975

THE ARTISTS

Tais Teng
Cover artist, After the Tsunami

We're delighted to have another Tais Teng painting for this issue. The giant bovine skull in a stark landscape visited by an oddly prosaic tourist family is the perfect accompaniment to our excerpt of Michael Kamakana's *Advent.* This is the fourth digital painting by Tais Teng that has graced the cover of *Pulp Literature,* the first three being *Youth Hostels of the Faery* (Summer 2014), *Pesky Summer Jobs* (Spring 2015) and *Dieselpunk Explorers* (Winter 2016). The Dutch artist has also written a hundred books for both adults and children. Readers of *Pulp Literature* will recall his story 'Growing up with your Dead Sister' in Issue 8. You can find more of his art at taisteng.deviantart.com and you can read more about him on his website, taisteng.atspace.com.

Hugh Henderson
Illustrator, Blue Skies Over Nine Isles

Hugh Henderson is an artist and scholar based out of Vancouver, BC. He trains with both swords and pencils to master his arts, but still finds time to hang out with friends and prove to all that he is a massive nerd. He is inspired by the wide offerings of internet webcomics and paperbound graphic novels, as well as cartoons and anime, and he hopes to inspire others with his work the same way. *Blue Skies Over Nine Isles* is an adventure on a new frontier featuring sinister robots and stylish heroes. Follow along at blueskiescomic.com.

MEL ANASTASIOU
In-house illustrator
Mel Anastasiou loves drawing for *Pulp Literature* because she loves the stories she illustrates. She draws in black and white, working from imagination and inspired by details from Renaissance compositions. You can find more illustrations, as well as writing tips and news about her books and novellas at melanastasiou.wordpress.com.

JM LANDELS
Illustrator, Allaigna's Song: Aria
JM Landels studied at the Cartoon Centre in London, UK, under David Lloyd (*V for Vendetta*) and Dougie Braithwaite (*Punisher*). Although she is a perennial doodler, she put down her pencils and brushes after giving birth to three children, but rapidly dusted them off when she realized *Pulp Literature* was going to be an illustrated magazine. She blogs sporadically at jmlandels.stiffbunnies.com.

HALL OF FAME

These are the heroes — the Patrons and Pulp Literati whose monthly support helped bring you this issue. Please lift your glasses and give them a rousing cheer!

The Inner Circle
Jenever J Utsey

The Landlords
Adam Fout

The Innkeepers
Ada Maria Soto
Dana Tye Rally
Ev Bishop
Roger & Anne Anastasiou
A Bursewicz
Kevin Harris

The Cicerones
Sandra Vander Schaaf

The Bartenders
Keith Rydstrom
Alana Krider
Richard Gropp
Margot Landels
Ron Graves
Susan Lefeaux

Kristen Mah
Corey Reid
Michelle Balfour
Robert Bose
Sharon McAuley
Victoria McAuley
Brighde Moffat
Dave Wayne
Scott F Gray
Abigail Bruce
Patrick Bollivar
Dietra Malik
Elaine McDivitt
Angela Dorsey
Joshua Pantalleresco
Jackie Jones
Shannon Saunders
Donna Saunders
Emily Lonie
Chelsea La Vecchia

The Regulars
CC Humphreys
Marta Salek

Rina Piccolo
Leigh Matthews
Kim Harbridge
KT Wagner
Harmony Neal
Jenny Blackford
Jain Cairns
Catherine McArdle
Adelene Ellenberg
Clarise Rivera Starr
Michael Barrie
Exprmntle
Tom Jolly
Dave Charpentier
Leo X Robertson
Kristene Perron
Akemi Art
Jennifer Timer

The Clientele
Kathy Denton
Ray Hsu
Melissa Hudson

If you would like to join the ranks of these worthies you can become a patron on Patreon at patreon.com/pulplit, or join the Pulp Literati through our website at pulpliterature.com/join-pulp-literati/.

MARKETPLACE

Books

Advent *by Michael Kamakana* We thought we knew what the aliens wanted. Think again. pulpliterature.com/advent

Allaigna's Song: Overture *by JM Landels.* Music, magic, and the shaping of a hero. pulpliterature.com/allaignas-song-overture

Paperboy: A Dysfunctional Novel *by Bob Thurber.* Photography by Vincent Louis Carrella. shantiarts.co/uploads/files/thurber_paperboy.html

Stella Ryman and the Fairmount Manor Mysteries *by Mel Anastasiou.* Trapped in a down-at-the-heels care home. You'd be cranky too. pulpliterature.com/stella-ryman-and-the-fairmount-manor-mysteries

Trolls *by Kris Sayer.* A comic guidebook narrated by a giant-spoon-wielding troll hunter. tatterhood.bigcartel.com

The Writer's Boon Companion *by Mel Anastasiou.* Thirty Days Towards an Extraordinary Volume. pulpliterature.com/subscribe/the-bookstore

Bookstores

Book Warehouse 632 Broadway W, Vancouver, BC V5Z IGI (604) 872-5711 bookwarehouse.ca

The Comicshop 3518 W 4th Ave, Vancouver, BC V6R IN8 (604) 738-8122 thecomicshop.ca

Myth Hawker Travelling Bookstore Canadian authors·Canadian content·small and independent press mythhawker.ca

Phoenix On Bowen 992 Dorman Rd, Bowen Island, BC V0N IG0 (604) 947-2793

Village Books & Coffeeshop 130-12031 First Ave, Richmond, BC V7E 3MI (604) 272-6601 villagebooks@shaw.ca

White Dwarf/Dead Write Books 3715 West 10th Ave, Vancouver, BC V6R 2G5 (604) 228-8223 whitedwarf@deadwrite.com

NEO-OPSIS.CA

Explore neo-opsis.ca for submission guidelines, issue and subscription purchases, advertizing rates, news, information, desktop images, art, reviews, industry links and assorted neat stuff.

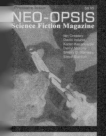

Use your WORDS

New Deadline!!

More $$$

Enter EVENT Magazine's
NON-FICTION CONTEST

$3,000 in prizes   5,000 word limit

Deadline: October 15

Visit **eventmagazine.ca**

Conferences and Events

When Words Collide 10 - 12 August 2018 Calgary, AB whenwordscollide.org

Surrey International Writers' Conference 18-21 October 2018·Surrey, BC siwc.ca

VCON 42 / Canvention 38 5 - 7 Oct 2018 ·Richmond, BC vcon.ca

Creative Ink Festival for writers, artists & readers 18-20 May 2018·Burnaby, BC Creativeinkfestival.com

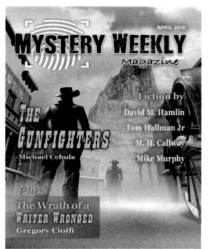

MAGAZINES

The Digest Enthusiast Explore the world of digest magazines, past and present, through interviews, articles, and reviews. Plus new genre fiction. larquepress.com

Geist Ideas + Culture·Made in Canada geist.com

Mystery Weekly Magazine The cutting edge of short mystery fiction www.mysteryweekly.com

Neo-opsis Canadian magazine of science fiction, based in Victoria, BC neo-opsis.ca

OnSpec The Canadian magazine of the fantastic onspecmag.wordpress.com

Polar Borealis Paying market for new Canadian SF&F writers & artists polarborealis.ca

Room Magazine Literature, Art, and Feminism since 1975 roommagazine.com

PRINTING & PUBLISHING

First Choice Books/Victoria Bindery Book printing & binding·graphic design· eBooks·marketing materials 1-800-957-0561·firstchoicebooks.ca

Wesbrook Bay Publishing Beverley Boissery author and publisher wesbrookbay.com

Dear Geist...

I have been writing and rewriting a creative non-fiction story for about a year. How do I know when the story is ready to send out?

—*Teetering, Gimli MB*

Which is correct, 4:00, four o'clock or 1600 h?
—Floria, Windsor ON

Dear Geist,
In my fiction writing workshop, one person said I should write a lot more about the dad character. Another person said that the dad character is superfluous and I should delete him. Both of these writers are very astute. Help!

—Dave, Red Deer AB

Advice for the Lit-Lorn

CONTESTS

Pulp Literature runs four annual contests for poetry, flash fiction, and short stories. For contest guidelines, prizes and entry fees, see our website, pulpliterature.com/contests.

The Raven Short Story Contest
Contest opens: 1 September 2018
Deadline: 15 October 2018
Winner notified: 15 November 2018
Winner published in: Issue 22, Spring 2019
Prize: $300

The Bumblebee Flash Fiction Contest
Contest opens: 1 January 2019
Deadline: 15 February 2019
Winner notified: 15 March 2019
Winner published in: Issue 23, Summer 2019
Prize: $300

The Magpie Award for Poetry
Contest opens: 1 March 2019
Deadline: 15 April 2019
Winner notified: 15 May 2019
Winner published in: Issue 25, Autumn 2019
Prize: $500

The Hummingbird Flash Fiction Prize

Contest opens: 1 May 2019
Deadline: 15 June 2019
Winner notified: 15 July 2019
Winner published in: Issue 21, Winter 2020
Prize: $300

$\mathcal{B}$ECOME A PATRON OF PULP LITERATURE!

By supporting *Pulp Literature* on Patreon with $2 or more per month, you will be laying the foundation for a secure future for the magazine, as well as ensuring you will never miss an issue! Your subscription includes four big issues of short stories, novellas, poetry, comics and novel excerpts delivered to your door or electronic mailbox each year.

Find us at patreon.com/pulplit
If you prefer to subscribe through our website go to pulpliterature. com/subscribe.

Or you can send a cheque with the form below to:
Subscriptions
Pulp Literature Press
8540 Elsmore Road, Richmond, BC V7C 2AI, Canada

Don't miss an issue!

❑ **Send me 2 years (8 issues) at the special rate of $90** (save $30)*
❑ **Send me 1 year (4 issues) for $50** (save $10)*
❑ **Send me 2 years of digital issues for $30** (save $9.92)
❑ **Send me 1 year of digital issues for $17.50** (save $2.47)

Name: _____

Address: _____

City: _____ Prov. / State: _____

Postal code: _____ Country:_____

Email: _____

❑ Payment enclosed   Make cheques payable in Canadian funds to S. Pieters.
❑ Bill me   Include email address for digital editions and Paypal
❑ New   billing, or subscribe at www.pulpliterature.com.
❑ Renewal   *for postage outside Canada add $16 per year in North
                        America or $32 per year overseas.

THe STranGe YOUNG man In THe DeSerT

MATTHEW 3; 14:1-12; MARK 1:1-9; 6:17-29;
LUKE 3:1-21; 7:19-23; JOHN 1:19-35 FOR CHILDREN

Written by Ronald Klug

Illustrated by Betty Wind

Concordia Publishing House

ARCH Books   611

COPYRIGHT © 1971 CONCORDIA PUBLISHING HOUSE, ST. LOUIS, MISSOURI
CONCORDIA PUBLISHING HOUSE LTD., LONDON, E. C. 1
MANUFACTURED IN THE UNITED STATES OF AMERICA
ALL RIGHTS RESERVED
ISBN 0-570-06057-5

In old King Herod's wicked days,
as Isaiah had foretold,
there appeared in the desert a strange
young man
with a voice that was strong and bold.

He wore rough clothes of camel's hair
with a leather belt tied round.
He ate wild honey and locusts for food
and slept in a cave underground.

He was not afraid in the desert wild,
because he trusted in God.
When people heard of the way he lived,
they thought him a little bit odd.

One day this John began to speak;
in the desert his voice rang clear.
From villages, cities, and neighboring towns
the people came out to hear.

John preached,
"It's time you changed your ways.
Repent, start doing what's right.
Come down to the river
and be baptized.
God's kingdom is coming
with might."
The people came,
and some of them
asked, "Tell us,
are *you* the King?"
But John cried,
"No! I'm not the One.
It's news
of Him I bring."

Then one day
Jesus, the King
walked by
and John said
"Look at Him
Behold
the Lamb of God is here
He'll take away your sin."

While John was teaching
on Jordan's bank,
Jesus came by to see.
"Baptize Me," said Jesus.
But John said, "What?
You should baptize me!"

Jesus replied, "Do as I say."
And finally John agreed.
He baptized Jesus there in the river,
and a strange thing happened indeed.

The Spirit of God came down from heaven,
came in the shape of a dove.
And the voice of God, like thunder, said,
"This is My Son, whom I love."

Then Jesus and John came out of
the water, and Jesus went on
His way. John kept teaching and
told the people all that had
happened that day.

Now old King Herod did a wicked thing:
he married his brother's wife.
Brave John told Herod that he was wrong
to live such a sinful life.

The king didn't like to be told
so he called his soldiers in.
"Go find this John, and throw
Enough of this talk about sin!

was wrong,

in jail!

John was captured, sat long in jail
till he wondered about one thing.
He sent some friends to Jesus to ask,
"Are you really Christ, the King?"

"Tell John to look at the things I do,"
said Jesus to the men.
"The deaf can hear; the lame can walk,
and blind men see again."

John's friends returned
to tell him the news
and listen to John's reply.
"I trust this Jesus.
He's God's own Son.
Now I'm not afraid to die."

King Herod invited his friends and lords
to a feast in his royal hall.
Salome danced as they ate and drank.
Her dancing pleased them all.

Her dance so pleased
old Herod the king
that he said,
"Now listen to this:
Salome can have
whatever she wants,
and if half the
kingdom it is."

But Herod was sad
when he heard her reply,
for she talked to
her mother and said:
"I want nothing less
than to have John killed
and for you to give me his head."

So John was killed,
and his good friends came
and buried him in a tomb.
They met and prayed
and talked and cried.
Their faces were
filled with gloom.

"What shall we do now?" they asked themselves.
"John, our leader, is dead."
They looked bewildered till one spoke out,
"Remember what John said?
'Behold the Lamb of God,' he said
as Jesus was walking by.
Let's go to Jesus, follow Him,
and serve Him till we die."

DEAR PAREN

This bo ... tory
of a strange ...

His bir ... the
aged priest ... will
bear you a ... s to
prepare the ... had
said.

His wa ... wild
honey for fo ...

His me ... ople
to repent an ... ing.

He was ... iself.
He pointed ... akes
away the sir ...

He was ... fe to
do what he ... King
Herod that ... fered
prison and ... thful
to God.

He see ... ot so
strange. He ... lked,
lived, and d ...

THE EDITOR